FOR LOVE OR LEGACY

Ruth Cardello

For Love or Legacy
by Ruth Cardello

website: RuthieCardello.com
email: Minouri@aol.com
FB: Author Ruth Cardello
Twitter: RuthieCardello

Also by Ruth Cardello:

*Maid for the Billionaire
(Legacy Series Book One)*

THE LEGACY SERIES:

BOOK 1: MAID FOR THE BILLIONAIRE

Dominic Corisi knew instantly that Abigail Dartley was just the distraction he was looking for, especially since having her took a bit more persuading than he was used to. So when business forces him to fly to China, he decides to take her with him, but on his terms. No promises. No complications. Just sex.

Abby has always been the responsible one. She doesn't believe in taking risks; especially when it comes to men - until she meets Dominic. He's both infuriating and intoxicating, a heady combination. Their trip to China revives a long forgotten side of Abby, but also reveals a threat to bring down Dominic's company. With no time to explain her actions, Abby must either influence the outcome of his latest venture and save his company or accept her role as his mistress and leave his fate to chance. Does she love him enough to risk losing him for good?

BOOK 2: FOR LOVE OR LEGACY

Nicole Corisi will lose her inheritance if she doesn't find a way around the terms of her father's will, but she will have to partner up with her estranged brother's rival to do it. As pretense becomes painfully real, Nicole will have to choose between Stephan or the family he is driven to destroy.

Stephan Andrade has been planning his revenge ever since Dominic Corisi unscrupulously took over his father's company. With Corisi Enterprises gambling its reputation on the success of a new software network for China, Stephan finally has his chance to take back his legacy. Dominic's younger sister, Nicole, asks Stephan for his help and provides him with an opportunity to exact his revenge on a personal level.

It all goes smoothly until he falls in love.

BOOK 3: BEDDING THE BILLIONAIRE
(COMING TO AMAZON, SUMMER 2012)

Lil Dartley's life is upside down. Her previously steadfast and predictable sister is marrying an influential billionaire and needs help planning the wedding of the century in less than a month. Years of middle class rebellion have not prepared Lil for handling diplomats or paparazzi.

Jake Walton knows a train wreck when he sees one. Lil was trouble from the first day he met her, but since her sister is marrying his best friend, he has no choice but to help her or this wedding will be in the news for all the wrong reasons. Teaching Lil how to fit into high society would be a whole lot easier if she didn't drive him insane both in and out of the bedroom.

BOOK 4: SAVING THE SHEIK

(Zhang and a sheik, just because the story is wonderful to imagine.)

DEDICATION:

To my step-daughter, Alisha—one of the strongest women I know and a big part of my own happy ending.

CHAPTER *One*

DEATH WASN'T SOMETHING Stephan normally celebrated, but this one had its perks.

"Is everything set for tonight?" Stephan Andrade asked without looking up from the screen of his laptop while he typed in one last sentence. He'd completed the final presentation himself, more than an hour ago, but wasn't satisfied with it. Nothing new there. He hadn't brought his family back from the edge of financial ruin by doing anything half-way.

"If by everything, you mean do I have my overnight bag packed and sitting under my office desk in case I go into labor while checking for the third time that your itinerary for the next few days is set? Then, yes," his secretary answered ruefully, easing her very pregnant body down onto his white Maxolta sofa and propping her swollen ankles up on one of its pillows.

"Good," he said absently, then stopped and rubbed the back of his neck with one hand when her words sunk in. "Maddy, you shouldn't be here today; you're on maternity leave. I could have had made the arrangements myself."

"You were already snapping at everyone in the office. I thought I should help out before you had a mutiny. If I didn't know how important this deal was to you, I would have called Uncle Vic and told him that you need a parental intervention."

His father would love that phone call. Victor Andrade was in his early sixties and had moved back to Italy, but that hadn't slowed him down. He flew across the Atlantic on a regular basis, enjoying his retirement in a villa on the Amalfi coast while keeping track of his family in New York. Luckily, Stephan's mother reeled her husband in now and then or Stephan would never get any peace.

"No need to involve my father; your husband already called me twice this morning," Stephan said.

That brought a smile to the brunette's face. Not a difficult feat. Madison D'Argenson was habitually, chronically, in a good mood. She said it was part of her charm. Luckily, she was equally efficient and detail oriented, or she would be a highly paid mailroom clerk instead of Stephan's secretary. She said, "He's supposed to be concentrating on the new restaurant opening, not worrying about me. The baby isn't due for another week. What did he say?"

"The usual threat—I'd better not work you too hard in your condition or he'll poison my next plate of tortellini."

His younger cousin laughed at that, but Stephan didn't join her. Her joy echoed through him, a hollow reminder of how much he had changed. He was only six years older than Maddy, but he felt ancient next to her.

Her enthusiasm could be exhausting. Unabashedly, she grabbed life with both hands and shook it until she got what she wanted, rewarding those around her with the sweetest smile that had probably ever graced the planet when she won, a smile that usually crumbled any residual opposition.

When she'd come home from a year of studying abroad in the South of France with an unknown French Chef in tow, Stephan had voiced his concerns and he hadn't been alone. On paper, Richard D'Argenson hadn't been impressive. Maddy's response? She'd gathered the family from brothers to cousins—and informed them that Richard was there to stay and that they would love him.

They were married in less than a year and pregnant soon after that.

Richard had won Stephan's respect by refusing to accept financial backing for his restaurants and for allowing Maddy to continue to work at Andrade Global. Even as a newlywed, Richard hadn't been put off by how protective the Andrade men were of their women. He was devoted without being controlling, and he fit into the family just as Maddy'd proclaimed he would. Most impressive was the fact that he was constantly learning traditional Italian cuisine from Maddy's mother so he could feed multiple generations of the clan at her parents' house each Sunday. How could they not love him?

Even when he threatened to poison you.

Usually it was amusing. Today, it was annoying. There was too much riding on this deal for Stephan to allow himself to get distracted. In just a little over twenty-four hours, he'd be pitching his proposal to China's Minister of Commerce, and if all went well, Andrade Global would be an international player, and the infamous Dominic Corisi would be scrambling to survive the financial fallout.

Maddy eased her feet back onto the floor and said, "I actually had a good reason to come in and interrupt you this time."

Stephan crossed the room and, with a gentleness that not many outside his family would associate with him, assisted his petite cousin as she struggled back to a standing position. "You really should go home, Maddy. Whatever it is can wait until I get back in a few days."

Yes, the deal was important to him. In fact, it was all he had thought about since he'd first heard that Dominic was going to make a bid to the Minister, but Maddy was family, and family, to an Andrade, was everything.

Maddy rested a hand on the sleeve of his jacket. "No, this can't. I'm worried about you."

"Me?" His head pulled back with pride.

"Yes, don't lose yourself in China, Stephan."

"I don't intend to lose." He knew by her wince that his tone had been harsh.

Not that it stopped her.

She said, "That's not what I mean and you know it." Her voice softened with concern. "Are you going to Beijing for the right reasons?"

Why was she doing this now? He checked his watch. About forty-five minutes until scheduled takeoff. It wasn't like his private jet would leave without him, but he had meetings lined up for when he landed and making them depended on getting there ASAP. "If Andrade Global succeeds in winning this contract -"

"What, Stephan? What will change? You've already more than made up for what your father lost..."

"My father didn't *lose* anything. It was stolen from him." She knew this.

"And China is all about making Dominic pay for that, isn't it?"

Oh, yes. "Dominic should pay for what he did to my father - for what he did to all of us. Isola Santos is a

4

mockery of what it once was. I've offered Dominic money for it many times, but this time I won't be the one asking. When I'm done with Dominic, he'll be *begging* for whatever I'm willing to give him in trade just to pay for the lawyers he'll need to sort out the mess I'll leave for him in my wake."

It felt good to say it out loud.

After all these years, Dominic had finally miscalculated and left himself vulnerable. By including influential investors from around the world in on his push to create a viable network for China, Dominic had put his personal wealth at risk. His investors were not going to be pleased at all when Stephan offered the Chinese government the same service for a third less cost, with more freedom to implement the restrictions they wanted. Unlike Dominic, Stephan didn't care if he had any control over the software once it was purchased. All that mattered was closing his rival out of that market.

"You don't have to do this," Maddy said urgently.

"Yes, I do." It was that complex and that simple. He put his hand lightly on her back and nudged her toward the door. "You worry too much, Maddy. I'll be back before the weekend. Just tell the little one in there that he or she has to wait for me."

Maddy refused to budge. "Stephan, I still have something to tell you and it's important."

He looked down with quick concern. "Is it the baby?"

Maddy placed her hand over her large bump. "No, the baby is fine, but I came in here to tell you that Nicole called earlier. She asked if you were here and if she could see you today."

"Nicole?"

"Nicole Corisi. Odd, that she would want to see you today, isn't it?"

"Yes, odd," he parroted, while his mind raced. What would Dominic's little sister want? He had been careful to keep the details of his planned coup under wraps until now. Only the closest members of his team knew what he was about to do, and half of them were already in China laying the groundwork for his presentation. Had information leaked to the Corisi camp? Did Nicole intend to ask him to back off her brother?

"I hope you told her that my schedule is booked," he said.

Maddy tapped a finger on her chin. "Her father passed away recently. I couldn't say no. Weren't the two of you friends at one time? Maybe she needs someone to talk to."

An image of Nicole dancing shyly before him in the dim lighting of Lucida's seaside balcony dance floor near Coney Island would not be denied; her long black hair blowing lightly across the cleavage her little red dress revealed. Those dark gray eyes laughing up at him in response to something he'd said. After months of chasing her, she'd conceded to one date. All his ribbing about how seriously she took herself and her attire had produced this deliberate, physical dare. Without her office armor, she was...*dangerous.* Her moves were inexperienced, but deadly all the same.

He'd never wanted a woman more than he'd wanted her that evening.

He never had since.

Perhaps if the night had culminated in the usual fashion, she might have faded into the blur of women he had known. But news of Dominic's bid for his father's company had come out that evening, ending whatever they might have had before it had begun.

Taking her from him. Leaving him with a feeling of something unfinished.

No they had never been friends.

On any other day, he would have met her — if for no other reason than to see if she could still affect his breathing with just a look. He'd be willing to indulge himself for a day, or a week, or however long it would take to get her out of his system.

Oh, yes, on any other day he wouldn't have minded comforting her.

But not today.

Not the day before he exacted his revenge on her brother.

"Although it is sad about her father, there is nothing I have to say to Nicole that she would want to hear," he said.

"You must be a little curious about what she wants."

"I don't have time for this." Stephan checked his watch again. "I've got less than an hour before I fly out. Call her back and tell her that I can't see her."

Maddy didn't move into action as he'd expected. Instead, she gave him one of those argument-melting smiles and said, "That would be a little awkward since she's sitting right outside the door."

Stephan rocked back first with shock, then forward as anger began to burn deep within him. He wanted to roar his frustration, but his cousin's delicate condition held his tongue. Later, there would be plenty of time to talk to Maddy about how she shouldn't interfere. She knew damn well he didn't want to see Nicole.

Get it over quickly and get out. "Two minutes. She has two minutes."

Maddy's smile only widened, revealing that she not only knew what he was thinking, but also that she wasn't afraid of him. She turned to walk back to the door and said over her shoulder, "Oh, and Stephan, she's even prettier in person than she is in the picture you keep hidden in your desk."

"HE'S AS READY as he'll ever be to see you," the very pregnant woman said with some humor to Nicole as she held the outer door to Stephan's office open behind her, one hand resting atop her well-rounded stomach.

"Thank you," Nicole responded stiffly and stood, mustering her resolve, but unable to make her feet move forward toward the door. The persuasive words she'd rehearsed on her way over flew out of her head.

He's never going to say yes to this. I'm wasting my time.

"Are you ok?" the woman asked, stepping away from the door and looking up at Nicole with concern.

You don't have to do this. Memory of the fervent plea made earlier that day by Thomas Brogos, her father's long time lawyer and friend, held her immobile a moment longer.

Yes, I do, she had answered.

Everything she loved, everyone she loved, depended on getting Stephan to agree to her outrageous request. She couldn't fail today.

"I'm ok," Nicole said even while her body betrayed her by threatening to increase the tears she kept blinking away. *No,* her mind screamed. *I'm not ok. Nothing is ok.* Nothing had been in a very long time and, if this didn't work, nothing ever would be again.

"I know this is none of my business, but I just want you to know that I'm out here if you need me."

8

Oh, God, I'm such a wreck that a pregnant woman is worried about me now? Taking a deep breath, Nicole willed her feet to carry her through the door and into Stephan's office.

Stephan Andrade, ex-spoiled rich kid, now corporate shark and owner of enough diversified computer software companies that no one was quite sure how his empire wasn't considered a monopoly, rocked back in his sleek office chair and steepled his fingers in a mockery of contemplation. Light from the immense office window behind him cast a shadow across his face, concealing any emotion which might have shown in his eyes. Manhattan's skyline cut a ragged silhouette across the horizon, as harsh and unforgiving as the man who had not bothered to stand when Nicole had entered his domain. An oversight and slight breach of etiquette for some, the lack of movement was nothing short of a slap in the face from a man who prided himself on his traditional old-world upbringing.

It didn't help that he was still gorgeous.

If life were fair at all, Stephan would have been rounder in the middle with a receding hairline. Several inches above six feet, he was a striking mixture of his Scandinavian mother and his Italian father — thick blond hair, eyes so blue they caught ones attention from across a room, and a natural muscular physique that most men spent hours in gyms trying to emulate. But life wasn't fair, and his good looks were just as necessary to ignore this time around as they had been seven years ago.

"Thank you for seeing me," Nicole said, the words caught in her throat. Nothing about his expression or his mannerisms implied that he would entertain her request. She wasn't about to turn tail and run, though, just because

9

he was looking her over like she'd tracked mud across his priceless rug.

"I am flying out of town in less than an hour. What do you want, Nicole?" His voice implied that whatever it was, the likelihood that she was going to get it was close to zero.

Ever so carefully, Nicole sat on the unforgiving, white chair before Stephan's desk. She smoothed the knee of her navy pants suit and crossed her ankles to one side, hoping she didn't look as anxious as she felt. "Can't you at least try to be civil, Stephan?"

The jaded man who sized her up now bore little resemblance to the young man who had visited his father's company frequently over several months for no other reason than to saunter through her office, looking like he'd just returned from surfing, and ask her if she'd go out with him. She'd always said no, and he'd always smiled as if her refusal had just made him like her more.

He wasn't smiling now.

He stood and walked to the front of his glass desk. "We both know this isn't a social visit. I'll admit I'm surprised that your brother stooped to sending you. His deal must be in worse shape than I thought."

Nicole clutched the purse on her lap. "Dominic didn't send me."

Stephan leaned back, crossing his arms across his wide chest. Despite his expensive tailored suit and silk tie, he looked anything but tame. He had clawed his way from near bankruptcy back to the front page of financial magazines and the experience had hardened him. "Riiiiight," he drawled.

It doesn't matter what he thinks of me. "I need your help," she said.

His eyes narrowed while he weighed her statement. "You needed something and you thought of me? How touching. Did you consider the time we haven't spoken and the circumstances of our last conversation before you came here?"

"You know I had nothing to do with what happened."

A careless shrug of his shoulder volleyed that he knew no such thing.

"Stephan. I don't even talk to my brother. I hate him. If I had known that he was going to buy..."

"Steal..." Stephan interjected.

"If I had known anything about what was going to happen, I would have tried to stop him."

"Easy to say now."

"What do you want me to say, Stephan? I went to him when it happened. He wouldn't listen to me. I tried to apologize to your family. What more do you want from me?"

"I guess the real question is - What do *you* want from *me*?"

Nicole shut the door on the welling response from within her. He wasn't asking her what she had once wanted, what she'd spent many lonely nights dreaming could happen between them. He didn't want to hear about that foolishness any more than she wanted to resurrect it. No, today was about something much more concrete, and the only thing she still allowed herself to care about. "My father left me his company, but he named Dominic the acting CEO for a year."

Stephan barked out a laugh. "Genius. Dominic was the one sabotaging your father's company, it makes sense that he's the one to turn it around."

11

"Do you know what Dominic will do with the company as soon as he gets his hands on it? He's going to fire everyone at the top and put his own people in there."

"And?"

"And I can't let that happen."

"Because you need to be in control."

Does it matter? He wouldn't believe her. He'd made up his mind about her a long time ago. "I just need to know if you can put the past aside long enough to help me."

No didn't require vocalization; it shone in his ice-cold eyes and the stiff set of his shoulders.

"I can make it worth your while," she added quickly, playing her last card in this game.

He pushed off from the desk. Suddenly interested. "Now this I have to hear."

It would slow the rebound of the company, but if Stephan didn't agree to help her, she was going to lose it all anyway. "I own the patent to a new conversion software. I could sign it over to you."

He leaned closer. Close enough that she could smell the light scent of his aftershave. Close enough to block out her view of everything but him.

"Disappointing," he said.

"What is?" She shifted uncomfortably in her seat. Beneath her modest navy jacket and silk blouse, her body was having some very immodest reactions to his nearness. She didn't want to remember how those lips, the ones that were so close that she could lean forward and taste them, had felt on her neck, on other parts that were now straining against lace - begging for his attention.

She met his eyes and realized that he was watching her reaction intently; testing something, something they both knew was there, something that was better left unsaid.

She steeled herself against her need for him. Hadn't she learned years ago how giving in to a whim, even if only for one evening, could have devastating emotional consequences? Losing him would never have hurt as much if she hadn't allowed herself that one day of believing that she could actually have someone like him in her life.

"Your offer. I thought you had something a little more *personal* in mind..." he said. One corner of his mouth curled at the thought.

Calm. Breathe. Stephan would pounce on any weakness. Not that she hadn't imagined that pouncing - in glorious, tantalizing detail - but not here, not like this. "Trust me, nothing personal is being offered."

"What a shame. I would have almost been tempted." His suggestive smile was a flash from the past that elicited an instant, completely unexpected playful response from her.

She said, "Who are you kidding? You would have been panting at my feet." And regretted the words as soon as they were uttered.

His eyes lit with a spark of interest so intense that Nicole had to look away before she completely forgot all the reasons they could not give in to that attraction. He laid a hand on either arm of her chair suggesting her escape relied on revealing what she was trying very hard to deny. "See, that is what always intrigued me. Which one is the real you? The cool bitch who talks about her recently deceased father only in terms of his will or the much more tempting tease who just threw down a challenge? What would you do if I took you up on it?"

His words gained the reaction he'd likely desired. Her head whipped back around, only to find that he was closer, much closer than she was comfortable with. He might want her, but he'd wanted many women over the past seven years. The tabloids were full of pictures of him with some heiress or starlet on his arm. No one held his interest for long, and Nicole couldn't risk the pain of losing him a second time.

He leaned in just a fraction closer.

"I don't know why I said that," she said, back peddling.

"You said it for the same reason I'm fighting to keep my hands off you. There is something between us; something we should have resolved years ago."

"I can't go there, Stephan." Her voice was huskier than she'd intended.

"I can't either, so you're safe." He straightened. "Go back and tell your brother that however tempting the offer is, I'm not going to call off my plans - not even for a romp with you."

And the truth rears its ugly head.

He didn't want her.

He'd only wanted to see how far she'd let him go.

Nicole said, her hands curling into angry fists, "You know, I'll never understand why you and my brother aren't the best of friends - you're both complete assholes."

"Tsk, tsk. Your mask is slipping. It'll be hard to explain to Dominic how his plan involved slugging me."

Nicole stood, chest heaving, and said, "This is all a game to you, isn't it? You just want to see if you can get to me." She hated that her eyes blurred with tears when she wanted to show him how little his jabs affected her.

What's the use? Why hide it? In a moment she was going to walk out that door and never see him again, anyway. "Guess what? You won." One tear escaped down her cheek. "I was an idiot to think that there was a shred of humanity in you."

She turned to leave.

"Nicole..." he said softly.

She turned back, her composure returning with icy calm. He wasn't going to seriously pretend to care, was he? Or had he just thought of another witty slam that he couldn't resist imparting before she left? "What, Stephan? Have you thought of another insult? Do you think that after the week I've had I really care what you think of me?"

Slowly, as if the words were wrung from him, he said, "You shouldn't have come here."

"That much is obvious, thanks," she said, turning away and walking toward the door only to stumble over nothing. *Dammit, can't I at least hold it together until I get out of here?*

He caught her by the arm near the door, stepping in front of her and waiting until she looked up at him. If she didn't know better, she'd have thought he was concerned.

"What did you think would happen when you walked through the door? Did you think I'd be overcome by old emotions and forget about everything else?"

She wasn't surprised that his words held some bite. Looking at him holding her arm, all of her anger left her. Really, what *had* she expected? "No. It's pretty obvious that whatever you felt for me is gone. I wouldn't have come if my lawyers had been able to find any other way."

"A way to what?"

Nicole met his eyes. "To break the will. A year ago, you made a bid for Corisi Ltd. My father initiated, but never completed, his acceptance of your offer so it still falls under unfinished business and therefore provides the only loophole my lawyers could find."

His hand tightened. "So, this is all about money after all."

Nicole shrugged sadly. "Does it matter? You won't help me."

His face tightened and his blue eyes raged with emotion she hadn't expected to see. No, she chastised herself. Now was not the time to imagine that he was unwilling to let her leave for the same reason she wished she could stay. Life didn't work that way. Not hers, anyway.

"What did your lawyers come up with?" he asked.

What do I have to lose? she thought. She said, "If you bought Corisi Ltd and sold it back to me, the company would be outside the control of the stipulations of the will."

He shook his head as if he'd heard her wrong. "Buy it? Buy a thirty million dollar company for you?"

If there was even the slightest glimmer of hope that he would help her, she couldn't leave yet. "It would just be on paper. It wouldn't end up costing you anything."

"Just my stock standing as my board and investors begin to doubt my sanity."

He hadn't said no — yet.

"I thought about that, too. No one would be surprised if..."

"If?"

She spoke quickly, getting her plan out before she had a chance to reconsider the wisdom of it. "If you and I were engaged. This would all make sense. When families merge, their companies do, too. It's natural. Then, when we call off the engagement, you sign the company back to me for the same price and you've lost nothing."

His expression was unreadable. "You've thought of everything except for why I would do it."

"That patent. Stephan, it shows real promise. It could make you millions."

For a moment, he looked like he was tempted, but then he said, "Even if I wanted to help you, no one would ever believe it. No one would believe we're engaged."

"They would if you said we'd been secretly dating."

"No."

"Engagements happen all the time. Tell people I'm pregnant. I don't care."

He raised his voice, "My family would lose their minds if they thought we'd been secretly dating — never mind engaged because you're pregnant. *No.*"

Did he have to sound disgusted?

A knock on the door. Maddy poked her head in. "Stephan, my car is here so I'm leaving."

Stephan checked his watch and swore. "Maddy, do me a favor and double check that mine is coming. It was supposed to be here ten minutes ago. I'm on a tight timetable."

Maddy looked back and forth between Stephan and Nicole. "Will do." She closed the door as if reluctant to do so.

Lost in his thoughts for a moment, Stephan stared after his departing secretary.

"Stephan," Nicole said.

"Hmm?"

"Let go of my arm."

He dropped it. "I don't hate you, Nicole. If you were asking me for a reference or...hell, even a loan, I might be able to help you, but this is too much."

"I understand," she said, composing herself and stepping back from him.

His phone vibrated in his breast pocket. He checked it quickly then said, "That's my car downstairs. I wish I could help you, but I can't. You're going to have to live with your father's will."

CHAPTER *Two*

WELL, THAT WENT worse than expected, Nicole thought as she exited the elevator and entered the main foyer of Stephan's office building. The click of her Louis Vuitton heels caught the attention of the men at the security desk. They both looked up and, in union, dismissed her with insulting speed.

Was there a flavor of ice cream that would make this day tolerable? Probably not, but Nicole had plans of testing out a carton or two that evening.

Her inability to gain weight was a gift and a curse. In her teen years, she'd sprouted to a couple inches shy of six feet, and without much padding, she'd looked like an awkward scarecrow for years, all arms and legs. Not someone men looked twice at. Age had softened the angles of her face, but the real curves she'd hoped for had never come. No need to buy sexy clothing when you don't have the assets to support them.

Not that the general lack of male attention bothered her. She'd poured herself into her studies and various internships over the years with one single goal in mind – saving her father's company. A goal that had never seemed further from her reach than it did today.

Dominic wouldn't care that the top executives had worked for Corisi Ltd for almost twenty years. The private company had survived a failing economy and deliberate sabotaging because of the loyalty and integrity of those very people. They were more than long term employees, they were the only family Nicole had ever known.

And she'd failed them.

"Are you ok?" Stephan's secretary asked as she stepped away from the lounge area and into the main foyer. Even pregnant, or maybe because of her condition, she held the attention of the security guards longer. Nicole envied the woman's natural confidence. Her ruched, plum maternity dress accentuated her delicate form and clearly celebrated her temporary figure.

"Yes, I'm fine," Nicole answered automatically.

"You don't look ok," the woman persisted.

Despite the difference in color, the woman's dark brown eyes reminded Nicole of Stephan. He didn't have a sister. Was she a cousin? Victor Andrade had always advocated employing family. Stephan might have kept up that practice. "Maddy, right? I appreciate your concern, but I've had a really rough week and I'd rather not talk about it."

Relief! Her limo was at the curb waiting for her. Nicole excused herself and headed out the glass doors.

Maddy followed her out onto the street as if she had something further she wanted to say. Nicole watched her struggle to catch up and reluctantly waited for her. She said, "I thought you were leaving a few minutes ago."

"I gave my ride to Stephan." Maddy grimaced. "Don't tell him. This trip is important to him and I thought I could wait for the service to send another car."

"But?" *Please don't have a reason I can't leave you here on the curb. Oh, God. Do you go to hell for thinking that about a pregnant woman?* Nicole looked around, hoping that an extra limo had miraculously appeared.

"But I'm not feeling so good." Maddy put one hand behind her to support her back.

Dammit.

Nicole waved for her limo to pull closer to them. He backed up and opened the door. "Why not sit for a minute? Do you want me to call your service again?"

Settling onto one of the plush seats on one side, Maddy said, "I'm sure I'll be fine in a minute. I'm just tired. The air in here feels great."

Wanting nothing more than to drive off and away from everything Andrade, Nicole stepped inside and sat across from the reason she couldn't. "Are you uncomfortable?"

Maddy rolled her eyes. "I am due in a week and shaped like an overblown beach ball. There isn't an inch of me that *is* comfortable."

They passed a moment of shared awkward silence.

Maddy winced. "Ooof."

"What is it?"

"I must have sat wrong at my desk because my back is killing me."

Shame on Stephan for having Maddy continue to work this late into her pregnancy. Was there *any* trace left of the gentler Stephan she'd fallen in love with so many years ago? Had he existed at all or had she projected what she'd wanted to see onto just another power-hungry suit? Little Maddy deserved better treatment. "Are you sure I can't call anyone for you? How about your family?"

"No." Maddy made a face as she had another back spasm. "I'll be fine as soon as I get home. I hate to ask you this, but do you think you could give me a ride?"

"You're welcome to take the limo. I don't mind catching a taxi." It would be a win/win. Maddy could get home safely and she could escape from what was turning out to be another awful day.

"Please don't. I mean, yes, I'll take the ride, but don't leave. I don't know why, but I feel funny about being alone right now."

What could you say to that?

Nothing but yes, especially if you were well acquainted with how being deserted felt.

"No problem, what's your address?" Maddy shared her uptown address and Nicole repeated it to the driver. They pulled out into traffic.

Maddy was the first to break the silence. "So, are you ok with Stephan going to China?"

Nicole clasped her cold hands in her lap. "What Stephan does is none of my business." A fact that was painfully clear after seeing him today.

"Do you know why he's going there?"

"Like I said, none of my business." She didn't want to be rude, but the last thing she wanted to do was discuss the man she was planning to spend the evening trying to forget.

"Even when it involves your brother?"

"Especially when it involves my brother," Nicole said, turning to look out the window.

"That must be hard."

"I'm sorry?" Nicole answered, continuing to watch the people on the street.

"Not getting involved. I don't think I could do…" Her sentence was cut short by another back spasm.

"Are you ok?" Nicole's family had consisted of just her and her father since her early teen years. She had no experience dealing with pregnant women, but Maddy was looking more and more uncomfortable. That couldn't be good.

"Yes, just some twinges. This happened a couple of days ago. It was false labor. I'm sure this will pass. Don't worry, even if it were real labor…this is my first, we'd have plenty of time."

Nicole's stomach twisted and she almost lost her lunch on the floor of the vehicle. She caught her breath and said, "Labor? You could be in labor?"

"I wish, but I'll probably be one of those first timers who go past their due dates," Maddy said with more confidence than Nicole thought the situation warranted.

Nicole tapped on the driver's window. "Jeff? Head to the hospital. Fast."

Maddy said, "I'm sure…"

The driver window lowered. "Did you say the hospital?"

"Yes, she could be in labor right now. How far are we?"

"Lenox is on 77th I think. That's not too far, but the traffic is at a crawl."

"Can you go around?"

"It's all backed up. There must be an accident. Nothing is moving."

Nicole took a shaky breath and then another. Shorter and shorter breaths until she felt a bit lightheaded.

Maddy said, "Breathe! Nicole, I'm not in labor." But she gave a small yelp and lost some of her confidence. "At least I don't think so."

Nicole could barely get a coherent sentence out, "You can't...you can't..."

Maddy raised an eyebrow.

Nicole finished lamely, "You can't have your baby here. I don't know anything about babies!"

Relaxing back into the seat for a moment, Maddy rubbed her stomach, but she wasn't sounding as calm as she had a few moments before. She said, "I'm sure this is nothing. Richard and I both panicked last time for no reason. I've taken all the classes. My water hasn't even broken yet. We're fine."

Nicole took out her phone and started searching the internet for imminent birth indicators.

Maddy joked, "Do you think there is an app for this?" But her joke was cut short by her first real cry of pain.

Nicole said, "You need an ambulance."

Wiping a sudden sheen of sweat from her forehead, Maddy conceded, "You might be right."

Not expecting her to agree, Nicole sputtered, "What do you mean I might be right? You said you were fine!"

Maddy looked down at the seat beneath her and said, "I think my water just broke."

"You think?" Her water just broke? The traffic was at a standstill. They were nowhere near a hospital. *Not good. Not good. Not good.* Nicole gasped for oxygen as her airway closed with panic.

Reaching across the limo, Maddy dragged Nicole onto the seat next to her with one yank. The sweet girl from earlier was quickly disappearing. She gritted her teeth and said, "Listen, one of us is going to have to remain calm here and chances are it's not going to be me. You're going to have to get a grip!"

What did they suggest a woman do during birthing? Short breaths? Nicole took several shallow breaths, then several longer ones. When she'd calmed, she was able to think somewhat clearly again. "You're right. I'm sorry. I've just never been around a pregnant woman before."

After quickly digging in her purse for her phone, Maddy called her husband. "Richard?" She broke off and exclaimed as pain tore through her. When it had passed, she said, "It's time. Head to Lenox. I know it's not what we planned, but it's the closest one. Yes, we're on our way. At least, we're trying to be on our way, we're stuck in traffic."

Nicole asked frantically, "Jeff, can't you get around these cars?"

The driver said, "We're locked in."

"What about a helivac?" Nicole asked, grasping for any solution.

"No place to land."

Breathing normally was getting more difficult again. "Oh, my God! Oh, my God! What do we do?"

911

Nicole fumbled with her phone, dropping it twice before she succeeded in making the call. She chose speakerphone because, like it or not, Jeff was going to have to listen in, just in case she passed out.

The dispatcher said, "911, what is the emergency?"

Nicole gasped for a breath and said, "We're having a baby. I mean Maddy is having a baby in my limo. She can't have the baby here."

"Ma'am where are you located?"

Nicole frantically looked out the window for signs. "We're on West 58th and 5th. In a black limo. The traffic isn't moving. You need to send an ambulance right now."

"Ok, ma'am, there is an ambulance several blocks away. I'm directing it to your location now. Pull over and wait for them."

Maddy screamed.

The operator asked, "How close are the contractions?"

Nicole looked at Maddy who was now reclined on the long seat, breathing in short bursts. "Maddy, how close are the contractions?" Tears started running down Maddy's face and she let out another short scream. *Oh, my God!* "I don't know. She's in a lot of pain. Should she be in that much pain?"

"Ma'am you're going to have to remain calm. Having a baby is natural, but can be extremely painful. You need to ask the mother how close her contractions are."

As the pain eased, Maddy finally answered Nicole. "They are very close. A few minutes, if that."

"A few minutes," Nicole said quickly into the phone. "Maybe less."

"Ma'am, you're going to have to prepare yourself."

"Prepare?" Nicole asked, feeling time slow with the shock of it all.

"The baby could come before the ambulance arrives. Unless anyone else is there, you're going to have to assist."

Nicole gave the young driver a frantic look, but he shook his head just as wildly and said, "Don't look at me. I pass out when I see blood."

"I don't think I can do this," Nicole said, panic closing in once again. She had never even applied a band-aide to anyone but herself, and this promised to be a whole lot messier than that.

Maddy said something into her phone then put it on speaker phone, "Nicole, it's Richard. He wants to say something."

"Nicole? Nicole? Are you there?"

"Yes," Nicole said, her hands shaking so badly, she almost dropped her own phone.

"You have two of the most important people in the world to me with you right now. Please take care of them." His love for his wife had a calming effect on Nicole.

Every once in a while, life threw you an opportunity to redefine yourself. You could either rise up to the challenge or live with the regret.

This is one of those moments.

I can waste time crying and hyperventilating myself into a blackout, or I can put on my big girl pants and stop thinking that this is all about me.

"I will Richard. They are both going to be fine," Nicole said and was surprised to hear the strength in her voice.

"Ma'am?" the 911 operator interrupted. "Do you have a place to wash your hands?"

Nicole shook herself out of inaction and assessed what was available. "The limo has a little bar area. I have hand sanitizer and bottles of water."

"Wash down quickly and then check the mother."

Nicole washed quickly, grabbed some fresh linen from the bar, and knelt to help Maddy out of her underclothes. What she saw almost sent her sprawling backwards onto the floor of the vehicle. "I think I can see the top of the baby's head!"

The pains were more frequent and increasing in intensity. Nicole put the phone down to help Maddy who was alternating between pushing and screaming. For what felt like hours, but was in fact only a sliver of that time, the operator called out advice that Nicole quickly followed. Nicole helped Maddy get as comfortable as possible and knelt on the floor, preparing to support the head and catch the baby.

It all happened quickly. First the head popped out, then the baby turned to one side, and suddenly a very slippery infant slid into Nicole's waiting hands. Nicole used one of the clean linens to wipe the baby's face and mouth. She wrapped it in another linen and laid it face down on Maddy's chest. The baby took its first deep breath and let out a wail.

Nicole wiped her shaking hands and laid out more linens on the floor. "It's ok! The baby is ok!" She was vaguely aware of tears pouring down her own cheeks.

The operator said, "The ambulance is on 6th now. You should be able to hear the siren in a moment."

Maddy was looking down at her new baby in wonder.

A male voice revealed that Richard was still on speaker phone, "Maddy? Nicole?"

Nicole answered, "The baby is fine, Richard! Can you hear it crying?"

"And Maddy?"

"She's still in some pain, but she's smiling."

"Is it a boy or a girl?"

Nicole realized she didn't know and laughed, "I don't know. I didn't look."

Richard said, "Should I worry that you couldn't tell?"

Nicole shook her head, then realized he couldn't see her and said, "No, all I cared about was that first breath."

Maddy peeked inside the linen and said in a happy, but exhausted voice, "Tell him it's a boy."

"It's a…"

Richard exclaimed, sounding like he was choking on a few tears himself, "I heard!"

The driver said, "Party's over ladies. The ambulance is here."

Maddy half-smiled and said, "Smack that man later."

Nicole smiled at her in relief, "I promise."

The limo was soon crowded with two EMS paramedics who moved Nicole over to evaluate the mother and child. Nicole stepped outside of the limo for a second. A crowd of people was gathering on the sidewalk speculating on what could have happened in the limo that required emergency care. Several pointed at Nicole. She moved away to hide behind the ambulance when she saw the first camera phone.

Her driver walked around the front of the limo and handed Nicole her phone. "The operator said you did great."

"I still can't believe it. Jeff, I just delivered a baby!"

"Yes, you did. And luckily you have more than one limo or we'd be using my Mercury this summer. I draw the line at cleaning that out."

That's what happens when you let the 22 year old son of your regular driver cover for his father for the summer. Unlike Arnold, who blended into the background as seamlessly as furniture and anticipated your every need, Jeff brought a bit more attitude with him.

Not that she could blame him in this case. "I'll ride in the front with you on the way home and we'll have it cleaned. Deal?"

"Sounds good to me."

I just delivered a baby!

Even though the experience was chock full of details she neither wanted to relive nor share with anyone, holding that new life in her hands and helping it into the world would forever rank as one of the most amazing events of her life. If she had a friend, she would have called them right then and shared her euphoria about the baby arriving with no complications for mother or child. Friends, however, were difficult to make and even harder to keep when you were a Corisi.

The only meaningful relationships she'd maintained into adulthood were with the top executives at her father's company. Unfortunately, she was no longer the little girl who could run into their offices and burst out with a story. They'd stayed in touch, even after she'd gone on to college and worked in various computer software companies in and around New York, but they were no longer part of her day to day life.

However, Nicole had never stopped being grateful for the years of kindness they had shown her when everyone else in her life had walked away. As she'd learned about business in college, she'd used what little influence she had with her father to improve their workplace. Surprisingly, she'd often gotten her way, not because it was best for the company and certainly not because her father valued her opinion, simply because her father knew that she would talk to him until he made whatever small concession she was asking for. He'd trivialized her interest as vanity, a need to leave her mark on what he'd created. Still, giving in had gotten him what he wanted — a reprieve from her presence; something he considered worth approving a few human resource initiatives. That knowledge never stopped hurting, but it had been useful when she'd sought childcare and flextime for those she cared about.

She would do just about anything for the ones she loved – even put herself at the mercy of a man who had once broken her heart. Admittedly, going to Stephan for help had been far fetched, but George and some of the other top executives had stood by her these past few weeks as her father's health had declined. They'd sat with her at the hospital, and had come to her house to make sure she was ok when her father passed away from a final heart attack.

They and their families had comforted her while her own brother had chosen business negotiations in Beijing over attending their father's wake and funeral.

They were all she had left.

"Ma'am?" asked one paramedic in a tone that implied he'd been unsuccessfully trying to get her attention.

"Sorry. Yes?" Nicole said, shaking off her thoughts.

"Are you coming in the ambulance with us?"

Nicole had barely opened her mouth to say no when Maddy raised her head, baby wrapped warmly beneath blankets on her stomach, and reached for her from the stretcher. "Please come," she said weakly and laid her head back on the pillow.

Concerned, Nicole looked at the paramedic who quickly assured her, "She's just tired, but I need to know if you're coming with or riding behind."

Nicole leaned over and gave Maddy's hand a supportive squeeze. "I'm coming with." To Maddy she said, "I won't leave you, don't worry."

STEPHAN RECLINED THE custom-designed seat his private jet and tried to close his eyes. He needed to be well rested if he was going to be on his game as soon as he hit the ground in Beijing. Dominic was not going to stay in the US long. Stephan needed to have a solid standing with the Chinese Minister and his council before Dominic returned if he was going to have any chance of pulling this off.

Several members of his team had been in Beijing for almost a month, laying the groundwork and cultivating the connections that would make this coup possible. Revenge doesn't require luck, just patience. Like a snake curling in preparation for a strike, Stephan had waited years for Dominic to slip up.

And he finally had.

Sleep was elusive. Stephan looked around the small cabin of the jet. It wasn't impressive by Corisi standards, but it gave him the advantage of speed. He could get almost anywhere in half the time of his flashier rival.

When Stephan closed his eyes again, all he saw was Nicole. He didn't need to torture himself with an old photo this time; she was back in all too vivid detail. Nicole in a hot little red dress. Nicole buttoned chastely up to her neck in her navy pants suit. Nicole deflating before his eyes when he told her that he wouldn't help her.

She'd been beautiful in her early twenties, but the woman she'd grown into was runway gorgeous, tall and lean with legs that went on forever. Her flawless features and her unusual dark gray eyes belonged on a magazine cover. Not that she seemed to care. Most women would have used their natural assets to gain the upper hand in situations, but Nicole attempted to hide hers beneath severe clothing.

And that damn black bun! It was just as tempting now as it had been when he'd fabricated every excuse possible to enter her office at his father's old company. It left her neck delectably exposed, itching to be kissed.

Stephan turned on his side and punched the pillow beneath his head. He had to stop thinking about her. He should be focusing on the reason for this flight.

Dominic was finally going to pay for what he had done.

Was it wrong to take advantage of his rival stepping away from negotiations to attend the reading of his father's will?

In most cases, the answer would be yes, but this was Dominic. His indifference was evidenced by his lack of attendance at the funeral and wake. Dominic had only returned to the US for the money he hoped he'd receive from the will. More was never enough for a man like Dominic. He had to have it all.

Had the situation been reversed, Stephan had no doubt that Dominic would have done the same. There was a bit of pleasure in knowing that taking advantage of someone's misfortune was a classic Corisi move. They were a ruthless bunch, bent on the destruction of not only their competition, but also each other.

In some ways, Stephan had Dominic to thank for his success in the business. Victor Andrade had been too old fashioned to weather the global market changes. He'd believed in long-term business relationships and maintaining a good reputation. His kindness had been his downfall. By helping, rather than buying out his competitors, he'd left himself vulnerable for corporate sharks.

On the other hand, Andrade Global was based on what Stephan had learned by watching Dominic's rise to power: *Morality is subjective. Take, don't ask. Attack the stronger, absorb the weaker. Accumulate enough so that you never have to apologize, and pay people well to clean up the mess you leave behind.*

It was a recipe for success that had made Stephan a billionaire.

But money and power weren't enough.

Nicole.

Dammit. This wasn't about her. It was about his family's island. It was about settling an old score.

And Nicole.

There was no way she was as innocent as she claimed. Her timing revealed her involvement. She'd infiltrated his father's company just before Dominic's forced buyout of it. And now, she'd thrown herself at him the day before he planned to take down her brother.

Ok, so she hadn't actually suggested anything more than a business deal, but it was pretty obvious that the whole engagement, the fake fiancé scenario, was a lie designed to distract him.

Did she have to look so sincere in her appeal? So saddened by his refusal?

So positively sexy in her indifference to him?

If only she had propositioned him and revealed her true nature; maybe then he wouldn't be fighting an erection each time he pictured letting down her hair, unbuttoning her collared blouse, and kissing the cool reserve right out of her.

There was nothing special about her. He knew plenty of beautiful women. She was merely a challenge, the intensity of which had been heightened by the length of time he'd wanted her.

Stephan crossed the aisle and got his laptop. Apparently, he was not going to sleep on this flight. He was also, damn well not going to spend it in some hormonal stupor just because he had seen her again.

Nicole had not belonged in his life seven years ago and she did not belong in it now. Sex would only complicate things more.

Even hot, wet, climax-until-you-can't-move sex.

He opened his laptop and stared at the start up screen, then closed it with a snap.

A pretend engagement to help her break her father's will? Insane! People don't buy companies and sell them back for no profit. She couldn't have imagined that he would even entertain her request.

Unless she was desperate.

Even so, refusing to help her had been the best choice.

The only choice.

He leaned his head back against the headrest and groaned as he remembered the tear that had twisted through his gut like a dull knife. Was it possible that her father's death had shaken her? Why was it important to stop Dominic from temporarily taking control of her father's company?

And the most painful question: *Will the great Dominic be able to save her company after his own empire comes crashing down?*

Why do I care?

I don't care.

Stephan put the laptop aside and reclined back in his chair again. He covered his eyes with one forearm.

This is going to be a long flight.

CHAPTER *Three*

MADDY WAS HANDED out of the ambulance on a stretcher to where her anxious husband was waiting. He took her hand, unashamed of the tears running down his cheeks.

A paramedic cautioned Richard to move, but the reluctant husband took another moment to plant a kiss on both his wife and the exposed forehead of his new son. One more gentle touch of the baby, as if making sure all was fine, and he allowed the medical staff to wheel Maddy down the hallway as he continued to hold her hand.

Alone, Nicole stepped down and out of the ambulance, feeling a bit dazed by the whole experience. She hadn't wanted to interrupt the reunion, but she wasn't sure what to do next. Should she stay? Should she leave? What did one do in this circumstance?

A middle-aged nurse touched her arm and asked, "Would you like to get cleaned up?"

Nicole looked down at the bloodstains on her pants, stains that even the dark material of her clothing did not conceal. She'd been so focused on the mother and baby that she hadn't noticed the dried blood that was still splattered up and down her arms. "Yes, please. I didn't realize…"

"That babies are so messy?" the nurse laughed as she led Nicole to a room where she could wash and change into scrubs. "The mother was lucky to have you there. We heard you stayed calm and did a great job with your first delivery."

Nicole started scrubbing down at the sink, grateful to have someone to debrief with about the experience. She said, "I was terrified," and realized how true that statement was as she said it.

The nurse turned her back as Nicole changed into the scrubs, but kept talking. "They say that courage isn't a lack of fear. It is doing what has to be done, despite your fear."

Nicole joined her when she was dressed and said, "I'll have to remember that saying. I like it."

"Ready to go?" the nurse asked, moving to open the door of the changing room.

Not really, she wanted to say, but didn't. She wasn't sure what she wanted. Her part in all of this was finished. Time to slip out a side door of the hospital and go home. She may have helped Maddy, but she didn't belong here with Stephan's family. The sooner she left, the better. Instead of sharing her thoughts, she simply nodded and followed the nurse back out to the emergency room entrance.

Nicole called her limo driver who informed her that he had arranged for a new vehicle and was already on his way, but lacking a siren, wouldn't be there immediately. Nicole headed back into the hospital's waiting room to get out of the late evening humidity. Sitting was a welcome relief.

A short time later, an older woman with a slight Italian accent approached her. "Nicole?"

"Yes?" Nicole answered unenthusiastically and stood, feeling drained now that she was coming down from the adrenaline that had been coursing through her. She was filthy and tired. The last thing she wanted right now was to be seen by anyone.

"My name is Elise Andrade, Maddy's mother. Richard told us you were here and I just had to find you to thank you for everything."

Oh, great.

Why couldn't it have been someone who knew my father? Someone I could give a fake smile to and run away from? Why did it have to be someone I used to dream of one day meeting?

"It's a pleasure to meet you. Congratulations on your new grandson." Nicole shook the woman's hand and accepted the double cheek kiss the woman pulled her down for. Elise was a petite auburn-haired woman with a waistline that hinted at a love of pasta. Her delicate features were framed by expertly shaped curls. The simple flowered dress she wore was comfortable, understated elegance.

Looking down at herself ruefully, Nicole supposed she should be grateful to have had time to clean up before meeting her. At least in the scrubs, she didn't look like an extra in a horror flick.

"How are you holding up?" the woman asked with genuine concern.

Nicole looked away, uncertain of how to respond. "Maddy did all the work. I'm just relieved that they are both ok."

A tall, dark haired man in a simple gray Fioravanti suit approached them. His hair was neatly trimmed in a traditional conservative style. The harsh lines of his face softened as soon as he saw the two women. "You found

38

her!" he exclaimed and enveloped Nicole in a hug that lifted her clear off her feet.

Elise laughed, "Alessandro, put her down. Nicole, this very enthusiastic man is my husband."

Once released, Nicole nervously smoothed her clothing back into place.

With an unabashed smile, he turned from Nicole to lift his wife in the same type of crushing hug. "*Tesoro*, I can't help it. I just saw the baby. He's so beautiful and he has my hair. Richard wants to name him Laurent, but I suggested Joseph after my father. Joseph, that could be a good French name, too, no?" He returned her to the ground, but kept an arm around her waist.

Elise shook her head in amusement. "Please excuse his manners. It's not everyday that we have our first grandchild and we are so grateful to you." She wagged a finger at her husband. "And let them decide on the name. Richard is French. If he likes Laurent we should respect his wishes."

"I won't have people calling my grandchild Larry. Now, Joe is a strong name. What do you think Nicole? Larry? or *Joe*?"

Nicole clasped her hands before her and said weakly, "I like both?" She looked over her shoulder, out the large window of the hospital, hoping to see her limo pull up.

"I still can't believe that Maddy didn't come to the hospital this morning when she first started to get pain. I told her to take them seriously, but children think they know more than their mothers," Elise said.

Nicole shifted uncomfortably. She tried not to think about her mother. It had been fifteen years since the morning she'd heard that her mother had deserted them, a day that was forever vividly etched in her memories. The mere mention of a mother released a tsunami of painful questions she'd never been able to answer. *Had she left because she wanted to or had she been taken from them? If she'd left Papa by her own choice, why hadn't she taken her children with her? Why hadn't she even said good-bye?* And the most painful question of all - *If she had stayed, would she still be alive today?*

"You must be exhausted," Elise said, sensing Nicole's change in mood. "Alessandro, have our driver take her home."

"No. No." Nicole said quickly. "He'll be here any second, but I appreciate the offer."

Alessandro said, "We must call Stephan and tell him that he picked a good woman to marry. You're a hero."

Nicole's stomach did a nervous flip. "Stephan and I aren't..."

Elise chastised her husband softly, "You were supposed to say nothing."

The large man shrugged as if it were of little consequence. "Si. Si. Maddy told us not to say a word, but surely it cannot be a secret now. Why would Stephan want to hide that he is marrying a woman we already love?"

Why would Maddy think...? She must have heard part of the conversation in Stephan's office. This was not good.

Elise said, "Maybe he wants to wait until the time is right to tell us."

Her words did not sway her husband. "And what did waiting do for Maddy? She had her baby in a limo, practically in the streets of New York. *Dios Mio*, Stephan is lucky everyone is ok. He should have stayed with her."

Elise threw one hand in the air and added, "He's not himself this week. You know how he gets about that horrible Corisi family."

Instantly realizing her faux pas, they both quickly looked at Nicole.

"I didn't mean…" Elise started.

"I understand," Nicole said. When you had a father whose ruthlessness in the business world was legendary, and a brother who was following in his footsteps, you got used to hearing your last name and profanity used interchangeably.

Awkward silence in five, four, three…

"Please. I spoke without thinking." High emotions brought quick tears to the woman's eyes.

The phone in Nicole's purse vibrated. "It's ok. It doesn't bother me, but I have to go. That's my ride."

Alessandro handed her the plastic bag that contained her soiled clothing, a bag she'd meant to throw away, but had forgotten to. She took it now, unable to meet the couple's eyes.

He didn't let go of the bag until she looked up at him. When she did, he said, "No one blames you for the sins of your father or your brother. Tell Stephan that. He doesn't have to protect you from us."

"I will," Nicole said, knowing full well that she wouldn't.

Protect me?

Nicole was pretty sure that was not what Stephan was going to feel inclined to do the next time they spoke.

NICOLE THREW HER bag of clothing into an outdoor trash bin before sliding into a very welcome open limo door. Once inside, she slumped into the back seat, slipping her shoes off and putting her feet up on the seat across from her.

Her driver, Jeff, turned in the front seat and asked, "Are you ok?"

Nicole snapped, "Why does everyone keep asking me that?"

Isn't it obvious? Jeff's expression seemed to say before he turned forward and started the vehicle.

Nicole took out a compact mirror and was instantly sorry she had. Her hair had completely escaped its clip. She smoothed a few areas that were standing straight up, but there wasn't much she could do with the tangled rampage of black hair without an elastic.

She caught Jeff watching her in his rearview mirror.

"Just take me home." Her brisk tone was meant as a warning, but Jeff remained unimpressed. He turned and simply stared at her, waiting. Jeff had his own set of expectations regarding driver/passenger etiquette. It was inappropriate, but his father, Arnold, had endured her teenage fits without complaint. The least she could do was tolerate his son for a few weeks. "Please," she added.

Satisfied, he turned and put on his seatbelt. After he pulled away from the curb and onto the main road, he said, "I've never seen you with your hair down."

She closed her eyes and sighed. "Do we need to discuss this? I know I look awful."

"Actually, you're hot. Who knew?"

Nicole didn't know what was worse - that her driver was commenting on her looks and she was too tired to correct him or that he sounded so shocked that she looked good.

Hot? Hmm?

Nicole pressed the button to raise the glass partition, but her lips curled in a small, reluctant smile. *I've been wasting money on stylists and designers when apparently all I needed to do was put my finger in an electrical outlet while wearing a potato sack. This is the look that works for me?*

Men are funny creatures.

CHAPTER *Four*

AN HOUR LATER, rinsing off beneath a warm stream of water, Nicole looked at her flat stomach and wondered if she would ever carry a life within her. And if she did, would anyone come to the hospital when it was born? How pathetic was it that the only people she thought might were somehow on her payroll?

Did Maddy fully appreciate what she had? Parents who loved her? A husband who cried for her? What would it be like to be an Andrade...or a D'Argenson as Maddy was? To be part of a huge extended family, surrounded by love, celebrated simply for being one of them?

It wasn't the first time Nicole had pondered this.

Seven and a half years ago, during an internship for the now dissolved Andrade Solutions, Nicole had visited their world. Stephan's father, Victor Andrade, perhaps moved by Nicole's earnest desire to learn the ins and outs of running a computer company, had taken her into his confidence. Unlike most people Nicole met, Victor had been neither intimidated nor impressed by her family's influence in the computer market. In fact, in the beginning, they had spent more time discussing his extended family than her job description. Someone was always getting married or having a baby. Andrade arguments were sometimes heated, but more often hilarious. The clan was huge and gathered for seemingly any reason. Victor's stories were addictive and foreign, like fairytales of some wonderful life Nicole could only dream of having.

Before long, Nicole shadowed Victor through most of his day. He let her sit in on important meetings and debriefed with her afterwards, often praising her on her fresh perspective. There had been gossip when she'd first joined his company that her loyalty might be with her father, but Victor had openly discussed this with her and believed her answer.

Nicole wanted to take over her father's company, but she wasn't looking to take over the world. She had a deep appreciation for the way Victor valued his staff and integrated his family into the company. It was amazing for her to see how his decisions were based on what was best for everyone — not just his wallet.

Victor's acceptance of Nicole had opened the door for her with the rest of the family. His wife, Katrine, had taken Nicole to lunch one Thursday afternoon and the two had enjoyed each other's company so much that it had become a weekly event.

Katrine was a tall, voluptuous blond with the same striking blue eyes as Stephan. It should have been easy to dislike her for that alone, but her warm personality diffused any jealousy. Although she didn't work for the company, she knew everyone in the office and her opinions were valued. In fact, her suggestions often became policy after a period of debate. She openly adored her husband and son, but that didn't mean she agreed with them. Watching Katrine and Victor argue over Stephan revealed a family dynamic so foreign to Nicole that she might have been watching a PBS special on alien cultures. They clashed, sometimes at high volumes, but their anger came and went like a flash of lightening in the sky. Points were made. Compromises were agreed upon. No harm done. Nothing festered. The Andrades were not afraid of offending each other, because they trusted the love that bound them together.

Nothing similar could be said for her family. Corisis were violent, vindictive, controlling, and unyielding on every point of consequence. The only thing they valued was the acquisition of wealth.

The Andrades had given Nicole hope. Corisi Ltd could be successful and still value its employees. Her future fantasy family could be loving and supportive. She was determined that her own children would never know the sting of loneliness or abandonment as she had. She told all of this to Victor, and he seemed to understand her as no one had before. He treated her more like a daughter than an employee. So, she'd never quite understood why Victor had frowned upon any interaction between her and his son.

Young Stephan. Hugely successful, if your definition of success was a deep tan and a frequent flier pass to the front page of the tabloids. He had spent most of his time on the west coast where he cultivated Hollywood friendships, made documentaries, and dated women with built-in floatation devices, returning to the East coast sporadically to visit his father and hold fundraisers for whatever environmental cause he thought was important that month.

Or as his father used to say — had been diddling his life away, instead of growing up and helping out with the family business.

Unlike his father, Nicole had thought Stephan was…well, perfect. Nothing bothered him. He dressed like a man on vacation, and had a presence that had to be witnessed to be believed. Women fought to catch his eye. Men envied his ability to take his wealth and influence for granted.

Nicole loved his idealism. Stephan used to talk about saving the world like he could.

After each time she refused his invitation to dinner, he would linger in her office, often sitting on the corner of her desk and telling her about his latest project. His passion for saving coral reefs or charting the rate some glacier was melting was inspiring and incredibly sexy.

Stephan's persistence had been flattering, but he changed women like some men changed their shirts. They were accessories he wore to one event and easily discarded for the next. Nicole refused him for the same reason she didn't buy lottery tickets. Unexpectedly wonderful things did not happen to her. They never had and she didn't have much faith that they ever would.

Which was why she still kicked herself for ever saying yes to Stephan.

For admitting to herself that what she felt for him was more than a crush.

For giving her family another chance to hurt her.

Nicole dried off and slipped on her long cotton nightgown and padded over to her bed. She didn't often allow herself the luxury of reliving that date, but tonight she wondered what life would have been like had Dominic not announced his takeover of Andrade Solutions.

She'd never forget the look on Stephan's face when he'd casually asked her out and, for once, she hadn't immediately refused. His blue eyes had lit with a fire that her body had instantly responded to.

To be wanted by a man like Stephan was something her virgin heart had no defense against. He'd leaned in, wiggled his eyebrows, and joked that the thrill of riding the Cyclone on Coney Island was just what someone like her needed.

"Someone like me?" she'd asked, half afraid of how he would describe her.

He'd sent shivers down her back by running a feather light caress up the lapel of her suit jacket and asking, "Do you ever let your hair down? Have fun?"

He'd made the word fun sound...positively erotic.

No, she'd never had *fun*, but the more he'd spoken the more she'd wanted to remedy that.

"Of course I do," she'd defended breathlessly.

"Liar," he'd whispered against her lips.

"Just because I don't want to go out with you, doesn't mean I don't go out with anyone."

Her comment had brought a delicious smile to his lips. "Really?" He'd caressed the exposed side of her neck with the back of his hand. "Who?"

She'd gulped, unable to think beneath his sustained attention. "Men," she'd said.

He'd laughed out loud and said, "I would hope that was your preference, or I really have been wasting my time." He'd stood up and challenged her with a request. "Spend tomorrow with me at Coney Island. We'll go on the rides. We'll walk on the beach. If you can survive being away from all of those other men for the entire day, I'll even take you to dinner."

She'd held her breath. Afraid to believe what she thought she saw in his eyes. "Are you teasing me, or are you serious?"

He'd leaned over, gently kissed her shocked lips and said, "Say yes and I'll show you just how serious I am."

Putting aside all the reasons she'd compiled for why it would be a bad idea, Nicole had said, "Yes."

His face had been adorably flushed. "Do you want me to pick you up at your house around 10?"

"No," Nicole had said quickly. "I'll meet you outside the office building downstairs."

"Afraid your father won't approve of me?" The idea had seemed to amuse him.

With a small, tight smile, Nicole had conceded, "Something like that."

Luckily, Stephan had accepted her answer and agreed.

Their date would remain so vivid in her memory that it would overshadow all the dates she went on after. Walking hand in hand with a man who couldn't resist stealing kisses from her each time an opportunity arose had made her feel like she'd stepped into a dream. A wonderful, passion-filled world where anything and everything was possible.

Whether he was talking about his plans for his next environmental documentary or retelling the latest Andrade drama, she couldn't take her eyes off him. He didn't give a whit about money or computers. His father was dead-on right: he'd had no interest in joining the family company. He'd studied film instead of business, and even though his documentaries hadn't gained him national acclaim, he loved making them and going on the adventures necessary to make them happen. He saw his wealth as nothing more than a tool that allowed him access to influential people who could help lobby for his causes.

He was everything she'd ever dreamt he would be.

On the seaside dance floor of Lucida's, she'd admitted the truth to herself.

I love this man.

Dinner had been an excruciating, prolonged exercise in foreplay. A kiss. A secret touch. A need that built until there was no denying how they both wanted the night to end.

Until Stephan's phone had rung and she'd watched him change into a stranger before her eyes. Dominic had made his bid for Andrade Solutions public. "Did you know about this?" Stephan had stormed. "Did you? Is that why you followed my father around everywhere, so you could report back to your brother?"

Maybe she should have defended herself. Perhaps, if she had explained back then about her relationship with her brother — or lack thereof — Stephan might not have turned on her. The less she said, the more furious he became. He'd yelled questions and accusations at her that she never did answer. As soon as his tone had risen, she'd shut down, barely registering what he'd said or the long cab ride home after he'd left her there at the restaurant.

It wasn't his fault.

He had every right to be angry.

He and his family were just more victims of her family's curse. Nothing good or wholesome lasted for long when it came into contact with a Corisi.

Looking back, Nicole could almost have stomached Dominic's actions had they been driven by a desire to protect her. But, no, Dominic had bought and dismantled the Andrade family company merely because he could, and because in doing so he had gleaned some financial benefit. His acquisition of the Andrade's ancestral island had seemed almost spiteful. He'd immediately begun construction of some ridiculously modern complex on it that was soon splashed across the covers of every architectural magazine, and effectively ended any chance Nicole had of mending the rift between her and the Andrade clan. Victor had accepted her apology, but Nicole had retreated from how powerless the sadness in his eyes made her feel.

She'd never gone back to see him, even though he'd said she was welcome. She couldn't bear the guilt and anger that filled her at the mere thought of seeing the Andrades again. Losing them was just one of the many reasons she would never speak to her brother again.

What would have happened that night with Stephan had the call never come? Would he have been like the man she'd finally lost her virginity to — more interested in the challenge of bedding her than anything else? Or like the few who had come after him, who had chased her in hopes of gaining some favor with either of the Corisi men in her life, only to leave her when they discovered that neither cared about her at all?

Had the connection she'd felt to Stephan been real or the product of an overactive and lonely imagination?

Like so many other questions she tortured herself with, it was impossible to answer.

The one thing she did know was that Stephan would never again look at her the way he did that night at Lucida's. The Stephan she loved was gone.

Nicole turned off the light, lying motionless beneath the coolness of her summer sheets. Maybe she should get a puppy or a cat, anything that would ease this...emptiness.

The energy of Beijing was invigorating. Stephan looked down at the crowded streets below his hotel room and mentally went over his list of last minute adjustments he could make to his proposal. Everything was clicking into place, just as he had planned.

The Minister of Commerce was entertaining his proposal and discussing it with his council. His sources informed him that Dominic's recent disappearance had shaken the Minister's confidence in Corisi Enterprises. Stephan didn't have Dominic's clout, but he had arrived at an opportune time with an extremely tempting offer. He would speak again before the Minister and the council tomorrow afternoon, at which time they said they would make their decision.

Nothing was going to stand in his way of finally showing Dominic Corisi exactly what it felt like to lose everything.

His phone vibrated with a text. "Good news at home, call as soon as you can."

He would call, but not until he had good news of his own to share.

And it looked like he would have some soon.

CHAPTER *Five*

JUST IN AND out.

Nicole stood in the short line of people who were checking in to do exactly what she intended to do — look through the thick glass of the maternity ward window.

It's natural to want to check in on the life you helped into the world. At least, that was what Nicole kept telling herself that morning as she buttoned up the jacket on her dark gray pants suit.

The hospital was busy, but Nicole was quickly called over to a previously-closed station. Money had its perks. Never waiting in line long was one of them. She knew her clothing and her carriage implied owner of the hospital more than it did stray woman sneaking a peek at a child she had no real business visiting.

"Name please."

"Nicole Corisi. I am here to see the D'Argenson baby in the maternity ward."

"Are you family?"

Her heart choked in her chest. "No."

"I'm sorry, I have instructions here for only family to be admitted at this time."

I knew I shouldn't have come. "Of course."

The woman appeared concerned. "Do you want me to call up and see if the mother would like to add you to the list?"

Nicole took a step back. "No. No. That's fine."

This was a stupid idea anyway.

She turned to leave when a nurse stepped in front of her. "Nicole?"

"I'm sorry do I know you?" Nicole searched the small blond's face for any hint of how she would know her.

"No, but you're exactly the way Maddy described you." She shook Nicole's hand warmly. "My name is Samantha. Are you here to see the baby?"

"No. Yes. I mean I was going to take a quick look just to see how he turned out, but I'm not family so it doesn't look like that is going to happen."

The nurse spoke to the woman behind the desk. "Print her out a pass. I'd say she counts as family. Not only did she deliver little Joseph last night, but she's also engaged to his uncle."

Words of correction formed and then dissolved on Nicole's tongue while the very friendly Samantha stuck the pass to her lapel.

"I probably shouldn't say anything. Maddy and I have known each other forever. She tells me everything and I think it's so romantic that you and Stephan had a secret engagement — but you never should have told Maddy. It's like calling the press. Who's your doctor?"

"My doctor?" *No, tell me it's not what I'm thinking.*

"For the baby? Will you have it here? Imagine how incredible that would be if you were there when Maddy had her baby and then she was there when you have yours!"

Nicole swallowed hard. *Yeah, incredible.* One might even say *impossible* since she hadn't had sex with anyone in over a year.

So much for Stephan's theory that no one would believe they were engaged.

"I'm on break for a few more minutes. I was hoping to see Maddy's parents, but I'll find them later. Come on, let's go see Maddy," Samantha said.

"Oh, I can't. I - I have an appointment this morning. I just dropped by to see the baby really quickly but that was a mistake. I should go."

Being Stephan's pretend fiancé had seemed like a good idea when it didn't involve actually looking anyone in the eye while she lied. And then, of course, there was the small issue of Stephan not yet knowing

It was probably better if she just left before…

"Samantha! Nicole!" Maddy's mother, Elise, called out from across the foyer and there was no evading her. She kissed Samantha warmly on both cheeks then greeted Nicole the same way. She held onto one of Nicole's hands as if afraid she'd slip away. "I'm so glad you're here. I was worried that I had upset you yesterday."

Apologies were not something Nicole was used to hearing, never mind accepting.

"It's forgotten already," Nicole said softly.

Elise tightened her hold on Nicole's hand briefly then smiled. It was easy to see where Maddy had gotten her charm from. "It should never have been said. Thank you for understanding. No wonder Victor and Katrine speak so highly of you. They are flying in this morning. When we told them that you were here, they said you had to come to dinner with us tonight. Please, say you'll join us."

Nicole's mouth went dry. "Stephan's parents are flying in? Do they know...?"

"That you're engaged? Alessandro could never keep that from his brother. You have made them both so happy. I think they are as excited to see you as they are to meet their new nephew." She turned to her husband and said, "Alessandro, could you check us in?" He waited in line about as long as you'd expect someone to who had paid for a new wing of the hospital – not at all.

Elise linked arms with Nicole, seemingly out of affection, but Nicole wondered what she would have done had she tried to pull away. On the surface, Elise was soft spoken, but Nicole didn't doubt that she was accustomed to meeting very little opposition.

Elise asked, "Are you coming with us, Samantha?"

Samantha looked at her watch and grimaced. "I've got to get back to my ward."

"You're welcome for dinner."

"I'm working a double shift today or I'd be there. Tell Victor and Katrine that I'll come see them this week."

Elise said, "We will. Bye." Then she turned to Nicole and asked, "Have you seen little Joseph yet?"

Nicole said, "Not yet. So, they chose the name Joseph?"

Elise rolled her eyes in amusement and motioned to her husband with her head, "They couldn't stand to see a grown man whine."

Alessandro didn't seem at all offended. He shrugged and explained, "Who is more likely to get picked on at school? A Joe or a Larry?" He stood so close that Nicole was half afraid he was going to crush her in a hug again. "Nicole. Explain to this woman that I am right."

As they walked down the hallway, toward the elevator, Nicole said, "I guess it depends where you live. I like both names. Laurent is a popular French name."

"Very diplomatic," Elise said. "Nicole knows better than to get involved in something that is none of her business. She's a smart girl."

"Don't tell me my family is not my business. My grandchildren getting beaten up in elementary school is my business," Alessandro said stubbornly.

Elise released her when they stepped into the elevator. She linked hands with her husband, easing his irritation with just a touch. Then she joked to Nicole, "I hope you don't expect to name your own children, Nicole, unless of course you pick a good Italian name. Andrade men brood over their children like little mother hens."

"Piccola madre gallina?" Alessandro growled softly down at his wife.

Elise simply chided, "Si, Alessandro. You heard me. You know it's true. Victor is the same. Two Italian mother hens, always butting into to their children's lives. When are you two going to learn?"

Alessandro shrugged, revealing that change was not impending. He winked down at Nicole as they stepped out of the elevator and into the maternity ward. "I like Joe better. They can make it Joe Laurent if they want."

Elise shared a look with Nicole that said, *You see your future?*

Nicole's stomach twisted with acid and nerves.

The more time she spent with them the more she remembered how easy it was to love them. Not a good idea considering that it would all come to an abrupt halt when Stephan found out. So far, she had neither lied nor worked very hard to correct the misunderstanding. She had to see

Maddy alone. If she explained the confusion to Maddy, she could hopefully inform the family and they would understand that the deception had not been deliberate.

LITTLE JOSEPH WAS with Maddy when they arrived in her room. There was barely any space for visitors in the mash of balloons and flowers that filled her hospital room. Elise and Alessandro took turns holding him then held him out for Nicole to take.

At first she shook her head, "I've never held a baby."

Maddy laughed. "Liar. You held him yesterday. And I guarantee that he is much easier to hold today. Just remember to support his head."

Nicole took Joseph into her arms gingerly. Yesterday, she'd looked at him through a haze of urgency and panic. Today, she saw how very small and delicate he was. She lifted one of his tiny fingers in amazement. He was gorgeous. Absolutely gorgeous. Thank God nothing had gone wrong. Nicole didn't realize she was crying until Elise handed her a tissue. "He's so beautiful," she said.

The proud mother and grandmother agreed.

Elise kissed her daughter on the cheek and said, "Your father and I are going to go get a coffee. Nicole can visit with you while we're gone. We won't be long."

After they left, Maddy said, "Thank you for yesterday. You were incredible."

"It was nothing," Nicole said, unsure of how else to respond. She handed Joseph back to his mother.

Maddy fixed the baby's cap with one hand and said, "No, you were wonderful. I will always be grateful for what you did."

Unable to hold it in, Nicole burst out, "You have to stop telling people that I'm engaged to Stephan! It's simply not true. You misunderstood what you overheard yesterday."

Maddy smiled serenely and said, "I didn't misunderstand anything."

Nicole said, "Yes, you did. I haven't seen Stephan in years. I came to him with some insane plan that he rightfully turned down. What you heard was part of that."

Maddy looked up from her baby and asked, "Nicole, do you love my cousin?"

No! –was what she wanted to say, but when she tried to voice the lie, she found she couldn't. Maddy knew the truth. She settled on honesty. "I used to think I did. I'm not sure I even like who he has become."

Maddy nodded in agreement. "Stephan needs you back in his life – now, before he goes too far."

Nicole said, "Too far?"

Maddy looked torn. "I've already gotten involved more than I should have, but I hate to see Stephan so unhappy. Aunt Katrine says he was never the same after losing you."

Nicole thought about Isola Santos and said, "I don't think it was me that he was so angry about losing. We only went on one date."

Suddenly confident again, Maddy said, "Will you do me a favor?"

Yes. No. Nicole finally said, "Depends on what you're asking for."

"Don't give up on a happy ending just yet."

Easy to say when you're sitting there with everything.

Nicole's throat tightened and dried. "Life is not a fairytale for most of us, Maddy. Not everyone gets what they want."

Maddy looked down at the baby in her arms and said, "They do if they are willing to fight for it. No one needs to know you're not really engaged."

"Stephan will be furious."

"Let him be angry," Maddy said.

Let him be angry.

Nicole had never heard four more empowering words.

She'd spent her life trying to keep the peace and where had that gotten her? Following the rules hadn't won her father's love. It hadn't brought back her mother or mended her relationship with her brother. Being apologetic and honest, hadn't even gotten her Stephan's forgiveness.

Nicole wasn't buying that Stephan was harboring some deep feelings for her, but Maddy was right about needing to fight for what you want. She'd accepted Stephan's refusal to help too easily.

Let him be angry.

He may not want to, but he is going to help me save my father's company.

Nicole excused herself to make a phone call. When she was sure she was out of earshot of everyone, she called one of her lawyers. "Draw up the paperwork necessary for Stephan to buy Corisi Ltd. No, he hasn't agreed to it yet, but he will. I have a plan."

CHAPTER *Six*

STEPHAN CHECKED HIS watch for the third time since he'd gotten word that Dominic had arrived and had gone in to meet with the Minister of Commerce. His own meeting with the Minister had gone well that morning, really well. Negotiations had hinged on how much control Stephan was willing to give the Chinese government when it came to censorship and distribution.

To beat Dominic, Stephan was willing to concede all control.

His lawyer, Robert Hynes, came into the conference room and his expression instantly put Stephan on edge. "You don't look happy," Stephan said.

"Dominic just offered five percent of Corisi Enterprise's profit to fund a scholarship program for rural women."

Rage filled Stephan. "And that closed the deal?"

"It sure did. The Minister signed the deal like he was afraid Dominic would change his mind. What are you going to do now?"

Good question. It wasn't easy to think past the throbbing anger bubbling within him. He said through gritted teeth, "It's airtight?"

"Looks like it. They are preparing a press conference now regarding the deal."

"I thought we had this one."

"We did, but this win might not have been Dominic's doing. Rumor has it that Zhang ambushed Dominic with the scholarship fund as part of the deal—giving him no choice but to sign it."

Zhang. He should have guessed she would be involved in this.

"I underestimated how much she wanted that to be part of the deal," Stephan said, kicking himself mentally for that miscalculation.

"We all did. At least you're out very little investment. If you move quickly, you can still corner the market in..."

"Haven't lost much?" Stephan roared. "Do you realize the international influence Dominic will now wield? Not to mention the financial force this will gain him. I just lost any chance I had of regaining Isola Santos."

Robert signaled with his hand for Stephan to calm down. "Don't shoot the messenger."

The messenger wasn't the problem. *Fuck, I should have seen this coming. How could I have gotten this close, just to piss it away?*

His lawyer said, "I refuse to believe that you don't have a plan B."

"I do, but..." He stopped himself from saying more. Regardless of what had happened today, he wasn't ready to go that far.

"It's illegal?"

"Do you care?" Stephan motioned for his staff to gather their belongings and head out.

Robert stayed beside Stephan and said, "Not as long as you make enough money to pay me to defend you in court."

Stephan laughed at that. Leave it to Robert to see this as an opportunity for business. "At least you say it like it is."

"Always, Stephan, always. Let's get out of here before the press descends."

At the sight of Dominic with his security detail, Stephan's lawyer said, "Dominic never leaves home without his militia, does he?"

"He needs it. I'm not the only one who wants to see him fail - and some of them are not as scrupulous as I am."

"You're a paragon of virtue. I've always said that."

"Why did I take you with me?"

"Because I'm the best and you wanted to win."

"Oh, yeah. How much extra do I have to pay for you to shut up?"

"More than you can afford. Hey, looks like your friend Dominic is having some trouble."

He was.

Why? The scene unfolding on the other side of the foyer was heated and one that Dominic looked like he wasn't fully in control of. "This, I have to see," Stephan said, stepping away from his friend.

"Be careful, Stephan."

Stephan glanced back over his shoulder and joked, "Are you charging me for this advice?"

Robert shook his head and slid his hands into his pockets, rolling back onto his heels with a small smile on his face. "No, it's free, but if you get tangled up in the Chinese legal system, that'll cost you."

STEPHAN STEPPED RIGHT into the mix of things. "I don't know how you always seem to squeak a win out in the end, Corisi. I thought I had you this time."

Dominic's muscles bunched and twitched beneath the tailored suit. "Are you behind this, Stephan?" he asked, his question a blatant threat.

Stephan quickly assessed the tension of everyone in the room. He studied Jake's defensive stance, Zhang's defiant tilt of the head, and the tears running down Dominic's girlfriend's cheeks. A slow, wickedly satisfied smile spread across his face. "I wish I could take credit for whatever is going on here, but unfortunately, this mess is entirely of your own making. For a man who just won, you look pretty miserable. That alone makes my trip here worth it."

Dominic took a threatening step toward Stephan, but his friend Jake interceded smoothly, "We wondered who was knocking on the back door. I should have known it was you."

Jake Walton, as polished as Dominic was rough. Stephan doubted Dominic would have gotten as far as he had in business without him.

"It wasn't easy staying off your radar, Walton," Stephan said. He added a jab he knew would get a rise. "You know if you ever decide to leave Corisi Enterprises, I could use a man like you on my team."

"I'm not going anywhere," Jake said and moved to stand shoulder to shoulder beside Dominic. How a man like Dominic could inspire loyalty from anyone was mind boggling to Stephan, but maybe it had more to do with dollar signs than personality.

"How touching," Stephan mocked. Luckily, this wasn't a social visit; it was an assessment. Dominic was hiding something.

Stephan turned his attention to the women in the room. Zhang Yajun, one of the few female billionaires in China, stood like a tiny warrior next to Dominic's little teacher friend. He should have included her scholarship fund program in his own proposal, but he had underestimated Zhang's commitment to it. "I can't believe you pulled it off, Zhang. This is the kind of coup they write about in the history books. Consider yourself welcome for dinner anytime. I'd love to hear the details behind today."

Zhang responded harshly, leaving little doubt in the room as to her opinion of the man addressing her. "Careful, Stephan. Water has been known to flood even the dragon-king's temple."

Ah, he'd almost miss her sweet disposition now that he'd lost the contract. Stephan shared his sarcastic amusement with Abby and said, as if speaking in confidence, "That's Zhang's way of saying – Go to Hell."

Abby Dartley, Dominic's newest conquest, was the buzz of conversation across the globe. This was the first time anyone had seen Dominic involve a woman in his business. A perfect opportunity to stir the pot a little and see exactly how vulnerable Dominic was when it came to his lover. Stephan walked closer until he was practically standing over her and smiled down with practiced charm. "Is this the little teacher who brought the great Dominic to his knees?"

Abby ignored his extended hand. "I don't know what game you're playing, but count me out of it."

He blatantly appraised her with a deliberate slowness that achieved his goal of fanning Dominic's fury. She was beautiful, but he preferred his women taller and thinner—edgier. An image of Nicole popped into his mind, but he shook it off angrily. She was not part of his life, and not even her memory belonged in this mix.

Still, Dominic's reaction was almost laughable and prodding him further was irresistible. "Are the tears for Dominic or because of him?" The growl behind him should have warned him, but he was intent on goading further. "He's never been one to treat a lady well. Although, I must say that, until you, I've never thought twice about his discards. You, however, have the world talking. I'd love to find out if you live up to what they're saying about you."

Dominic grabbed one of Stephan's shoulders and spun him just in time to meet the connecting force of his fist. Stephan stumbled backwards, grinning as he realized that his instincts had been correct—Dominic was not in control of the situation or himself.

Perfect.

Dominic glared down at Abby. "You can stop making eyes at him now, he's leaving."

Abby sputtered in defense. "I was not…"

Stephan's derision-filled laughter froze their exchange. "You're getting soft, Dominic, and that's what is going to make it easier to bring you down."

Dominic's hands clenched at his sides. "Laugh all you want, but after today, Corisi Enterprises will be a bit more difficult to screw with. We're out of your league, Stephan. You can't touch us now."

Can't I?

Plan B was beginning to sound better and better. "Don't be too sure about that, Dominic."

Dominic gripped him by the lapels of his jacket and hauled him forward until they were nose to nose.

Dominic's voice held a deadly calm. "Any hurt you might have incurred from me in the past was an unfortunate consequence of your poor business skills. In the future, it will be a bit more personal." He released Stephan with a powerful shove that sent him back several feet. "Get out of here, Stephan, before I stop caring about how killing you would affect this deal."

How dare he judge and dismiss my father's business skills? Devastating a man's life's work wasn't personal? Taking a family's ancestral island was just business?

What could be more personal than that?

An evil thought came to Stephan, the kind of thought that one would normally dismiss as too awful, if it were not hatched in the heat of the moment.

You want personal? How about sleeping with your sister?

It wouldn't really matter if his engagement to Nicole wasn't real—news of it would keep Dominic so off center that he wouldn't be watching his back. He wouldn't even know what hit him when he put his new servers online, only to have them crash again and again until the Chinese government threw him out by the scruff of his neck.

All he had to do was tell Nicole he'd had a change of heart. He'd *love* to help her.

Oh, yes, this was about to get very personal. He said, "No one is untouchable, Dominic. I doubt you'll be as smug the next time we meet."

Dominic nodded to his security.

Stephan bowed sarcastically, rejoined his group and left the foyer. *Let Dominic think he's won for now.* As Stephan and his team slid into the limos waiting outside, he chose to ride alone. He called a number he hadn't thought he would ever use. It was to a throw-away phone, untraceable.

"Mike. I've changed my mind. Do it." He read the security code off a small piece of paper that he'd kept tucked in his wallet.

There, it's done. Dominic's fate is sealed.

Surprisingly, there was no rush of pleasure at the thought.

Stephan hung up and dialed his father's cell phone. He could use some good news.

CHAPTER *Seven*

NICOLE COULD HEAR the voices inside the enormous mansion even through the closed door. Elise and Alessandro's home sat on top of a small hill, looking out over a reservoir like a Newport mansion, but with a more contemporary design. Only this family would own 34 acres of choice real estate property and adorn its pristine front lawn with a variety of tricycles and gym sets. Nicole raised a hand to ring the doorbell, but the door flew open before she could. A young boy, no more than five, sprinted past her and ran down the steps. His mother had a baby in her arms. She pointed to the escapee. "Can you grab him?"

Nicole looked down at her black Christian Louboutin sling back shoes and her cream colored pants suit and then at the boy who looked like he'd been playing in mud with his hands. Every other family she knew had nannies, but the Andrades didn't believe in them.

The boy stood, poised to sprint, just four steps below her. "Grab him?" Nicole asked, not really sure what that would look like.

The mother said, "Catch him. Net him. Hogtie him. Just bring him to the bathroom. He doesn't want to wash his hands before dinner."

The little boy stuck out his tongue at Nicole and took off around the corner.

Oh, the little stinker.

Nicole stepped out of her heels and gave chase.

She chased him around two parked cars, but he snuck past her and took off across the sloped grass lawn. The two were in a full run, when the little boy tripped going down a small incline and started to roll. Nicole pulled back to avoid stepping on him and also fell. They both rolled a few times in the thick summer grass before coming to a stop at the bottom of the small hill.

The little boy got to his feet first and peered down at her, accusingly. "You almost rolled over me."

Nicole tried to keep a straight face, "Sorry about that."

He stuck out a defiant chin, "I'm not washing my hands with Zia 'Lise's soap. It makes me smell like a girl."

"So, I'll have to hogtie you after all," Nicole said solemnly as if talking to herself.

The little boy tilted his head to one side in evaluation of her statement. "You're funny," he announced and offered her one of his muddy hands. Nicole took it and allowed him to believe that he was helping her stand up. He added, "And you're fast."

Nicole smiled. "Who knew?" She didn't let go of his dirty little hand. He was not getting away a second time. "Let's go back inside. I bet your mother is worried."

"I'm not -"

Nicole suggested, "What if we find some manly soap? I bet Uncle Alessandro doesn't like to smell like a girl either."

Elise came out the back door of the large house and wagged a finger at her nephew. "Matteo, come in the house right now. Look, you've gotten Nicole's pants dirty!"

Nicole looked down at her little captor and back up, and came to a quick decision. "It's not his fault. I was running down the hill and I fell. Matteo was just helping me up."

Elise nodded, knowingly. "Well, Matt, how lucky that you were there to help Nicole. Let's go get cleaned up."

Matteo looked up with pleading eyes. Nicole asked, "Elise, do you have ivory soap? I'm allergic to scented soaps."

Elise cocked a curious eyebrow at Nicole who merely shrugged. "Sure," she said. "Follow me."

Matteo said, "Sorry about your pants, Nicole."

Nicole said, "It's ok." And it was. She looked down at the stains on her left knee and knew that her pre-dinner adventure would likely be told and retold as a new Andrade family story, and there was a certain amount of pride in that.

Matteo said, "Want to race later?"

Nicole realized that he was now holding her hand rather than the other way around and her heart did a funny sort of summersault in her chest. "You're on."

And together they went into the bustling house.

VICTOR ANDRADE TAPPED his wife's arm and stood the moment Nicole entered the house. Nicole froze in the foyer, hardly noticing when someone slipped Matteo's hand out of hers and led him off to get cleaned up.

"Nicole, you came!" Victor said in a welcoming tone she'd never heard in her own father's voice.

Katrine kissed one of her cheeks and hugged her like a mother who hasn't seen her child in too long a time. Nicole stepped back and almost fell. Katrine grabbed her arm at the last moment and steadied her. "It's good to see you, Nicole."

Stephan's father walked over and Nicole stiffened in anticipation of what might be another awkward embrace. Instead, he stopped and simply touched one of her cheeks. "It only took my son seven years to come to his senses."

Nicole couldn't meet Victor's eyes. "His anger was justified. I…"

Victor's hand dropped and his jaw clenched, his voice raising with emotion. "You did nothing wrong."

Nicole shrank a little without realizing it.

Katrine said, "Victor, you're scaring the poor girl. Nicole, don't mind my husband's mood, he's upset with himself, not you. We were overjoyed to hear that you and Stephan had made up." Then she linked arms with Nicole and said, "Come on, Nicole, Elise is in the kitchen and she's been talking about you all day. She'll be thrilled that you came."

Nicole allowed herself to be led away.

Much to Nicole's amazement, Elise was actually cooking. The large kitchen contained several ovens and heating elements on a center island. Every area seemed to be in use. Apparently, Nicole did not hide her shock well, because Elise asked, "Do you cook, Nicole?"

Once again, Nicole felt like an unprepared outsider. She shook her head. No one she knew cooked. They *had* cooks. Cooking was messy and in general considered a waste of time by those in her small circle of acquaintances.

Elise asked, "You never cooked with your mother?"

Katrine jumped in quickly and said, "Elise, you know…"

Elise went pink, then rushed to Nicole's side. "I forgot, Nicole. You must think I'm a horrible person. I keep saying the wrong things around you, when all I really want is for you to feel welcome."

There was no doubting the sincerity of the older woman. Nicole said, "I do feel welcome and please don't worry. I wouldn't be here if I didn't enjoy your company."

Katrine said, "Isn't she everything I said she was? She's exactly what Stephan needs."

This time Nicole blushed.

As if sensing Nicole's discomfort at continuing to be the topic of discussion, Elise answered the questions Nicole wouldn't ask. "You're wondering why we don't have someone cook for us, aren't you? We often do. If it's just Alessandro and me, our house cook will throw something together for us. And Richard makes the Sunday feast. But tonight was special. When the family gathers, the food is part of the love, no?"

Nicole shrugged awkwardly.

Elise explained, "The sauce is my grandmother's recipe. The meatballs are Alessandro's mother's. Katrine makes her Norwegian lefse bread and everyone eats it. When we blend our food, we blend our families and old recipes keep those people alive in our hearts. You understand?"

There was little point in lying. "Not really, although it sounds beautiful."

Katrine said, "Don't worry, Nicole. I had no idea how to cook Italian food before I met Victor. Elise taught me everything I know."

Nicole walked around the kitchen, looking into the various pots.

Katrine added with a smile, "So, you either help us cook, or you do the dishes."

Wide-eyed, Nicole swung around, and Elise laughed out loud, "You are so bad, Katrine. We *do* have house staff. She's only teasing you."

Squaring her shoulders, Nicole decided she was up for the challenge. She'd delivered a baby for goodness sake. How hard could cooking be? She slid off her cream jacket and rolled up her sleeves. "Ok, where do I start?"

Katrine and Elise exchanged a blatant look of approval. Elise said, "All that is left now is desert. We always make a fruit crostrata in the summer, a kind of pie. Victor and Alessandro love them." Elise pointed to a bowl of peaches and plums on a nearby counter and said, "If you peel the fruit, I'll make the pastry for it. Then there should be blueberries in the refrigerator if you don't mind rinsing them."

Busy following her instructions, Nicole asked, "So, is everyone gathered tonight to celebrate the newest addition to your family? Too bad Richard and Maddy aren't here."

Elise walked over and patted Nicole on one shoulder, "We will celebrate Joseph's birth this week when he comes home from the hospital and Stephan has returned. Tonight is about someone else."

Nicole looked from Elise to Katrine, afraid to hope, afraid to care.

Katrine said, "Tonight is about you, Nicole. Welcome home."

Nicole had never felt so wonderful and so awful at the same time.

Amid the gregarious discourse that was part of having three generations of Adrades gathered around one table, Victor's phone rang. He held a hand up and the room quieted. "It's Stephan."

He listened to his son for a moment then said, "Yes, I know, it's all over the news that Dominic won the bid, but it's for the best, Stephan. I'm surprised you went to China at all. Why? I'm looking at why. Nicole is here with us. It's time for you to come home and focus on what is really important." A red flush of anger filled the older man's face. "What am I talking about? I'm talking about this foolishness with Nicole. You put her in an awkward position of lying to us when you asked her to keep your relationship a secret. She deserves better than that. My future grandchild deserves better than that."

Victor shook his head in response to something Stephan said. "And what is this about buying Corisi Ltd without even mentioning it? It's the right thing to do, but why the secrecy?" Victor didn't give Stephan much time to explain before he said, "You're right, we will talk about this more when you get home. Be sure of that. And don't dawdle in China. You have a new nephew waiting for you. Oh, yes, and you're lucky everything worked out with that, or even hiding in Asia wouldn't save you from Richard. Maddy had her baby the night you left. Thank God, Nicole was with her. You should have been. You should have made sure she got home safely."

Stephan responded with something that calmed his father somewhat.

Victor spoke with one hand waving in the air for emphasis. "She's fine. Everybody is fine. Your Nicole took care of Maddy. I'm not so happy with the details, but I'm glad you finally came to your senses and asked her to marry you."

Nicole held her breath.

"Now that is the first good idea you've had in a long time. Here she is."

Listening to an influential businessman being lectured by his father like he was an errant twelve year old was humorous, but Nicole wasn't fooling herself into thinking that Stephan was going to be anything less than furious with her. She took the phone and held it to her ear, careful to reveal nothing in her expression.

"Hi, honey," she said, half gurgling with a nervous laugh.

"What part of no did you not hear?"

"I miss you, too, honey, but we aren't alone right now. Your whole family is in the room with me."

"Be very careful with my family, Nicole. Very careful."

"Oh, don't worry. They're all thrilled at the news."

"Apparently." He was quiet so long that Nicole began to worry that the connection had been lost. When he did speak, the sarcasm was gone from his voice. "Did you really help Maddy?"

"I didn't have much choice. She decided to have your nephew in the back seat of my limo."

He sounded shaken. "And they are both really fine?" His concern for his cousin was moving to hear.

"They are. Your family is planning a celebration for little Joseph early next week. Will you be back by then?" Nicole sounded more nervous than she meant to.

"Worried that I will and everyone will find out that you're a liar?"

"Not really."

"You sound pretty confident about that."

"Yes. I figure you're at least a teeny bit grateful to me now," she said.

"You're right."

Nicole sat down with the phone. "I am? You'll help me?"

"It seems like the least I can do, everything considered."

"Oh, Stephan, thank you." *Wait, that's too easy.* "You really don't mind everyone thinking...I mean knowing that we're engaged?" A few heads turned quizzically toward her, reminding her that she'd have to watch what she said.

"No, I've decided that your idea has...potential benefits."

Sex? Nicole swallowed the question just in time. All eyes and ears were still on her. "I'm not sure what you mean."

"You will," he said in a tone that sounded more than a little suggestive.

Nicole hung up and handed the phone back to Victor. She said, "He says he'll be back early next week."

Alessandro said, "You must be so happy."

Nodding slowly, Nicole picked up a fork and nudged the food that suddenly had lost its appeal.

Stephan was back in her life.

CHAPTER *Eight*

I COULDN'T HAVE planned this better.

Nicole might have his family fooled, but she was not as innocent as she pretended to be. He wasn't quite sure how Nicole and Maddy had ended up in the same limo and he was grateful that Maddy hadn't been alone, but that didn't change what had clearly happened next. Nicole had used that event to infiltrate his family and give credibility to her claims of their engagement. She didn't care if his family was hurt by her eventual departure. All she cared about was maintaining control of her father's company, proof that she was every bit as greedy and unscrupulous as her brother.

Good, otherwise I would have felt guilty about using her.

Their fake engagement meant that they would be seeing a lot of each other over the next month or so. *Oh, yes.* The thought made him instantly hard. Sure, she threw insults at him and claimed to want nothing more than his help, but the heat in her eyes when she'd looked at him had given her secret away.

She wants this as much as I do.

Why not use this opportunity to finally get her out of his system? If he played this game right, he could soon walk away from two Corisis with the knowledge that they had both gotten exactly what they deserved.

Nicole wasn't like other women he knew. No amount of flattery or gifts was going to get her to lower her defenses. Like overtaking a well-protected fortress, this was going to require some strategy.

Everyone had a weakness, a secret, some motivator they often weren't even aware they had—something that unconsciously drove their daily decisions. You could get most people to do almost anything you wanted if you could discover what it was.

I must remember something useful.

Nicole liked her routines. From the conservative pants suits she wore everyday to the way she couldn't concentrate unless her stapler was in its proper place on her desk, she was a creature of habit.

Like Dominic, she would probably act impulsively when she wasn't in control of a situation. All he had to do was shake her up just a little and she'd fall into his bed.

And he knew just how to do it.

ALREADY UP AND dressed in a gray pants suit, Nicole answered the intercom at her father's house in the Hamptons. They hadn't had regular staff in over a year, since her father hadn't wanted anyone to know that his health was declining.

"DA Plant's Moving and Storage."

"Who?"

"DA Plant's Moving and Storage."

Nicole turned on the driveway video surveillance camera. The man speaking into the intercom sure looked like a mover. The logo on his blue uniform matched the one on the side of the truck behind him.

"I'm sorry, you must have the wrong address."

"We were told you might say that, Miss Corisi. Your fiancé sent us."

"I'm sorry about the confusion, but he shouldn't have called you. I'm not going anywhere."

The man wiped his forehead with his sleeve. "He said you might say that, too. Did you want him to cancel his appointment with your lawyer?"

Service with a threat. How nice. "Well, I didn't know movers were so verbose."

"He paid us extra for the message." The man sounded apologetic.

Oh, what the hell. The important thing was that Stephan had agreed to help her.

She pressed the button that opened the gates at the end of the long driveway.

Two movers hovered at the doorway as if not wanting to dirty the white marble floor, their wide eyes taking in her father's less than subtle display of his wealth. If it wasn't ancient or one of a kind, it wasn't worth displaying. Nicole snapped, "Come on in. What else did my fiancé say?"

The two men entered slowly. One removed his hat as if the great hall deserved an act of respect. "He said that you don't have to take everything, just enough for now."

"What does that mean?" she asked, not hiding her annoyance.

"I have no idea, ma'am. We'll just pack whatever you'd like us to."

"He has no right!"

One of the men backed up at her tone and almost knocked over a 2,000 year old roman vase.

"Watch out," Nicole said automatically, "That was my father's -" and she stopped.

It was all her father's. Everything in this house was his because it had all been for show. He'd paid someone to decorate every room with only the rarest and most expensive items from around the world, never allowing the house to become a home. And that roman vase? She'd never touched it, because he'd never let her.

She picked it up and smashed it on the floor at her feet.

Shards of ceramic flew in all directions.

It felt good.

She walked over to the Cycladic Greek figurines on the mantel and smashed each one on the floor, along with a photo of her father shaking hands with the President of some foreign country—a picture that should have been of her winning one of her early dance recitals. However, those pictures had been discarded with the trash, not valuable enough to put on display.

"Are you ok?" one of movers asked.

"I'm fine!" Nicole caught herself just before she reached for another priceless figurine. The two men were openly gaping at her emotional display.

It's an uncomfortable moment when you realize that there is a crazy person in the room and it's you. Nicole smoothed her hands down the side of her jacket and collected herself.

"What would you like us to pack?" one of the men asked nervously.

She looked around. "Nothing. There is actually nothing here I want." And she walked out the front door.

JEFF, HER DRIVER, lowered the partition on the way to Stephan's penthouse. He asked, "You really took nothing?"

"Nothing."

"Not even an overnight bag?"

"I told you, there was nothing there I wanted."

"You might want a toothbrush eventually." When she glared at him, he said, "Just saying."

His words sunk in. "I probably do want a toothbrush." She laughed, but not because it was funny, just because her life was completely out of control and she didn't have the faintest idea of how to put it all back together. She couldn't even make the smallest decision, like anticipating what she'd need at Stephan's. "I don't know what to do," she said out loud.

"Don't you have millions and millions of dollars?" Jeff asked.

Nicole shrugged. Her father had always kept her on a strict allowance. There had been rules to follow, and appearances to maintain. Money had never given Nicole the freedom so many people assumed it would.

Jeff continued, "Buy a new toothbrush. Buy a gold one. Buy whatever the hell you want."

He was way too personal, way out of line.

But he had a point.

Her father wasn't here to stop her. She might be fighting for control of the company, but she certainly had control of her own checkbook now. She could buy a lifetime supply of toothbrushes if she wanted.

There was just one problem.

"Where do you buy them, Jeff?"

"A toothbrush?" His surprise was not a compliment.

Instantly defensive, Nicole snapped, "I'm not an idiot. I know you buy them at a pharmacy or something. I've just never..."

"Never?"

It was mortifying to admit the truth. "The basics were always there. Our staff bought them. I didn't have to go shopping. Everything came to our house."

"That explains a lot."

"What is that supposed to mean?"

"Do you like what you're wearing?"

Nicole looked down at herself, "I never thought much about it. I've always dressed to..."

"Blend in?"

Nicole stiffened with anger. "I don't need you to judge me."

"I'm just telling you that I understand." Jeff didn't seem the least bit put off by her snarl.

"I doubt very much that you know anything about me."

He met her eyes briefly in the rearview mirror. "I know that your father was a controlling and angry man. I know that your mother deserted your family—or died—or did both when you were thirteen. Your brother clashed with your father over her disappearance so he left you, too, and was in a not-so-private war with your father until the day he died."

"Ok, enough. So my private life is not very private. I get it. What's your point?" *Really, could this day get worse?*

The sympathy in Jeff's eyes only made Nicole cringe more.

He said, "You're not the only person to experience abuse or loss. You should talk to someone about it."

"Like a shrink? Or a nosey limo driver?"

He shrugged, "Either. Both. I just can't sit here and watch you fall apart without telling you that what you're going through is normal. You survived an abusive parent, now comes the hard part." Nicole gave him no encouragement, but he didn't seem to require any. "Finding out who you are without him."

What if I'm no one?

"And I do that by buying my own toothbrush?"

"It's a start. Then we have to do something about your clothes. You look like a rich librarian."

How rude! "Wow, you really know how to build a girl's ego up. Most drivers worry more about the road than their boss's attire."

"What are you going to do? Fire me? You don't even pay that well."

"I don't?"

"No, you don't, and your father never did."

Just add that guilt to my tab.

"Then why does your father stay?"

"Because he likes you. He says you are like a flower in the middle of a thorn bush: not your fault you are there; and almost impossible to save."

Is that how people saw her? As a helpless victim? Someone who needed to be saved? No wonder she was alone. "I don't want to be that person anymore, Jeff," she said and realized how deeply she wanted to make that change.

"You're young, you're beautiful, you're rich. What's stopping you?"

A huge weight lifted off her chest. Nothing was stopping her. Absolutely nothing. "So, where does one go shopping when they don't want to look like a librarian anymore?"

84

"With your credit limit, *anywhere they want.*"

EXHAUSTED AND EXHILARATED all at the same time, Nicole dropped several bags down inside the door of Stephan's penthouse. She felt years younger in her new blue polk-dotted Oscar de la Renta dress. She was used to concealing what she had always considered boney shoulders, but she refused to hide anymore. As she'd entered the building, she'd caught a couple of men turning to give her a second look. Her heart skipped a beat and she wondered if Stephan would feel the same when he saw the new her.

She turned back to Jeff who was almost not visible beneath the packages he was laden with. She asked, "Do you believe in happy endings?"

"As in happily ever after?"

"I guess."

"That's not reality, Nicole. Life doesn't stop when the book ends."

"But some people find love and stay together their whole lives. A love like that's possible, right?"

"My parents have been married for 40 years. That's what they are celebrating this summer with their extended vacation. Dad still gets the biggest kick out of Mom's humor. So, yes, it's possible."

"How do you think they do it?"

"Why are you asking, Nicole?"

"Stephan and I had a real connection once."

"And now?"

"I want to believe it's possible to find that again, but men don't stay with me, Jeff. Why don't they stay?"

"Why do *you* think they don't stay?"

Nicole shrugged helplessly.

Jeff put the packages aside and said, "Listen, I don't know your history with men." Nicole opened her mouth to share, but Jeff raised a hand and added quickly. "And I don't need to, but from what I know about Stephan I wouldn't suggest you throw yourself at him. He won't respect anything he gets easily."

Nicole chewed her bottom lip. "He might not even be interested."

"He moved you into his penthouse. He's interested. Just be careful."

STEPHAN'S PENTHOUSE WAS a disappointment. Sure, it's location near Central Park had likely cost him well over twenty million, and the interior was modern and spotless, but it reminded Nicole of the stark house she'd just escaped.

Where were the photos of Stephan's family? Every decoration had been perfectly placed to balance the room. She'd been hoping to find something of the old Stephan within these walls. *Nothing.*

A short tour of the other rooms did not make Nicole feel any better. She went back to meet Jeff in the living room. He was seated on a couch whose crisp lines and modern white design did not appear to provide any comfort. *Just like my father's house, all for show.*

"The penthouse only has one bedroom. Just where does he think I'm going to be sleeping?" Nicole asked, as much to herself as to her driver.

Jeff rolled his eyes.

So, you think it's going to be that easy, Stephan? Move me in, enjoy yourself for a few weeks, then toss me aside like every other woman you've dated?

I don't think so.

She walked over and opened the door to his home office again. "Do you still have the number to those movers, Jeff? I'm not done shopping yet."

CHAPTER *Nine*

IT WAS PRETTY obvious that she hadn't heard him come in. She was standing on top of a small chair, attempting to bang a nail into the wall with the tiny heel of a shoe. The image of her bare shoulders, hair loose down her back, olive cotton sundress — simple, yet mouth wateringly sexy at the same time. And completely unexpected.

What was she up to?

Her slim hips swayed slightly to the music blaring through the penthouse. He had to say something. In fact, the longer he said nothing, the more scenarios his imagination came up with for how to quickly get that little sundress off.

He stepped into the room and turned down the music.

She jumped, nearly toppling from the chair. He caught her just in time, pulling her against him and letting her bare feet slowly slide to the floor. He could have let her go, but when she looked up at him, he saw a memory in her eyes— a memory of another time and place when he had held her this closely.

"I didn't think you'd be home until tomorrow," she said breathlessly.

"I left earlier than expected."

"I hope you don't mind that I made a few changes."

She referenced the room behind him as if he'd noticed anything but her when he'd walked in. He hadn't seen her with her hair down and in a dress since…

"I don't mind at all," he said as his hands naturally found the small of her waist and settled her more fully against him, not caring if she could feel what her nearness was doing to his body.

Her acceptance of the situation was exciting, even if it came with a twinge of disappointment that the chase was over before it had begun. She was already here in his arms, her nipples already pushing against the thin material of her cotton dress, eager for his attention.

The next few weeks were going to be exhausting, but oh, so pleasurable.

He swooped down to take her lips, but she turned her head to the side and his kiss fell on her cheek. His head drew back with a frown. He hadn't fallen victim to that move since third grade when his first crush hadn't reciprocated his affection.

And he didn't like it.

She pulled out of his embrace and took a few steps away from him. "I think it's a good idea, Stephan, to discuss some ground rules."

"Ground rules?" he growled.

"Yes, so no one gets confused."

"I'm not confused." He moved closer.

She moved further away. "This arrangement is strictly business."

"It doesn't have to be."

"I'm only here to save my father's company. In a few months, we'll be out of each other's lives again."

"Even more of a reason to take advantage of this time together."

"I don't agree, and that's why I converted your home office into a second bedroom."

My office? He stalked to the door of a room he normally banned everyone from and whipped it open. Sure enough, his black and gray office furniture had been replaced by an explosion of white and lavender, feminine crap. On one side of the room, a small twin sized bed stood where his desk had. She'd even repainted the walls white, with what looked like a flower stencil near the baseboards. "What the hell did you do with all of my stuff?" he yelled.

Nicole didn't so much as flinch.

"Everything that looked important was boxed and sent to your main office. The rest was put in storage. Isn't that why you sent the movers? So I could make myself at home here?" Her innocence sounded a bit calculated.

He'd underestimated Nicole and that was incredibly hot. Excitement drove his blood along with all of his irritation clear out of his head. He wanted to lift that dress and taste her right there on her new chaste linens.

"How long do you really think you'll be sleeping in there?" he purred.

Instead of coyly pretending not to understand or retreating, Nicole surprised him by stepping closer to him. She stopped just before their bodies touched. Close enough that he could feel the heat of her skin. Slightly above a whisper, she said, "If you want to sleep with me, Stephan, you'll have to do a whole lot better than cheap come-ons and well worn lines. In fact, you'll have to do something that probably isn't even possible."

90

Sheer willpower stopped him from pulling her that last half-inch that separated them.

Their mutual attraction slowed time for a moment, until the only thing that existed was the two of them. She raised a hand toward him and his entire body tightened instantly in expectation of her caress.

God, he wanted her.

He was ready to promise whatever it would take to get her into his bed.

Her playful, dismissive pat on his cheek took him completely off guard.

"You're going to have to get me to like you," she said and pushed a stunned Stephan back a step, out of her room, and closed the door.

LEANING AGAINST THE inside wall, Nicole let out a shaky breath. The shocked look on Stephan's face had been priceless. He probably didn't get turned down often. His ego could use the trim.

Would playing hard to get give them the time they needed to rediscover their old connection or would he lose interest and move on to someone else? For once, the uncertainty didn't scare Nicole.

The challenges Nicole had faced and overcome recently had left her feeling empowered. Regardless of his feelings, she'd convinced Stephan to help her. Corisi Ltd and its top executives would soon be safe. As soon as the paperwork was completed, she could start pulling her company out of the red, and show everyone that she wasn't some helpless, tragic victim who needed rescuing.

She'd won.

She'd finally won.

The confidence it gave her allowed her to look inward with more strength. Her past was a part of her, but it would only rule her if she let it. She refused to settle for being the sum of everything that had happened to her. It was about time she figured out exactly what she needed to be happy and fought for it.

That might mean rediscovering love with Stephan—if he was ready for something real.

Or it might mean leaving him in her dust.

Either way, she was taking control of her life.

Watch out, Stephan. It's all or nothing, and I'm done playing by other people's rules.

CHAPTER *Ten*

STEPHAN WAS NOT in a good mood the next morning. Falling asleep had been damn near impossible until the wee hours of the morning, and waking to see not a trace of Nicole in his penthouse irritated him.

And it shouldn't - which only irritated him more. Stephan padded from the shower to his bedroom closet in a towel. He chose what his father would call one of his "power suits." In less than an hour, he'd likely be knee deep in the legal jargon when he met Nicole at her lawyer's office.

His mood went from bad to worse when his phone rang. *Dominic? He must be getting desperate.*

As soon as Stephan answered, an accusation boomed out of the telephone. "What the hell are you doing with my sister, Stephan?"

"I don't think you want the graphic details."

Dominic hissed out an angry breath. "Why is she at your house?"

"Shouldn't you ask Nicole? Oh, wait, she won't take your phone calls. She hates you as much as I do. That has to hurt. "

"You're a new kind of low, Stephan."

"Maybe, but at least I don't kidnap my women." Oh, yes, he'd seen the news. The debate finally declared Dominic an over-the-top-romantic, but Stephan knew the truth. The little school teacher had never stood a chance against someone like Dominic. He felt sorry for the woman who had tried and failed to escape him.

Nicole was different. *She's using me as much as I'm using her.* "Your sister happily moved into my penthouse," he taunted.

"Leave her out of any vendetta you have against me."

Why, Dominic, you sound almost desperate.

How does it feel?

Wait, because it's going to get a lot worse.

"I can't. You haven't heard? We're engaged. That makes us practically family, Dominic."

"I'm going to kill you."

"Just be a man and don't send your goons. Unlike some, I don't hide behind security. But I guess someone like you, someone who collects enemies like others collect coins, would have to."

"You're not going to win, Stephan. I'm going to crush you. "

"Is that any way to talk to your future brother-in-law?"

Dominic was voicing some new threat when Stephan laughed and hung up. He had Dominic exactly where he wanted him—furious and distracted. By the time he went back to check on his coveted new software, it would be too late.

Stephan headed to his home office, only to remember that it was now a bedroom and swore.

Normally his instincts were dead on when it came to reading people, but every time he thought he knew what Nicole would do, she did the opposite.

The only thing about her that he was one hundred percent certain of was that she monopolized far too much of his thoughts.

NICOLE PRETENDED NOT to notice when Stephan entered the outer office of her uptown lawyer. She turned a page of the women's magazine that she'd stopped actually reading the moment she'd seen him exit the elevator.

You would have thought Stephan was a movie star by how flustered the secretary became when he addressed her. Who could blame her? He belonged in a calendar gracing any month that represented HOT. He didn't even have to get undressed to make women drool. He had the kind of animal magnetism that worked on the female libido regardless of what he wore.

Nicole turned another page of the magazine.

That was part of Stephan's problem. He expected women to fall at his feet.

"Nicole," he said as he stood above her, about a foot away.

"Oh, Stephan. You're here. Great, I told the secretary not to announce us until you arrived."

"I expected to come here together."

Poor Stephan. He didn't look very happy about being ditched. Nicole fought back a smile. "I had a few places I needed to go this morning." She laid the magazine down and stood, watching Stephan's reaction and hoping. The dark blue dress she'd chosen for the day was perfectly acceptable for a business meeting, but it also hugged her lean frame and left just enough of her legs exposed that she felt sexy in it. Another perk of having money was that with one phone call she'd found a makeup artist who was willing to meet her that morning and give her some tips on how to subtly accentuate.

The effort proved worth it. Stephan leaned down and whispered in her ear, "You look incredible in that dress, but I'd love to see you out of it even more."

She looked up at him from beneath her now long lashes and teased, "Has that line ever worked on a woman?"

He went a sudden shade of pink. "Yes," he said defensively.

And she burst out laughing at the expression on his face.

He didn't share her humor.

Nicole didn't gloat long. Stephan leaned forward, his hot breath tickling her ear before his words did, "So, that dress isn't for me? You didn't imagine how my hands would feel as I slid..."

Further conversation was halted by the inner door of the office opening and Gavin Burke, Nicole's personal lawyer, coming out to greet them. Despite the interruption, it took a moment for Nicole to shake the image Stephan had whispered. Her skin quivered in anticipation of his hands sliding her already short hem higher, cupping her, pulling her against him. She prayed the light flush that spread across her chest would go unnoticed.

Gavin took both of her hands in his. He was several inches shorter than Stephan, but attractive in a cute-boy-next-door-moves-to-NY-and-becomes-a-corporate-lawyer sort of way. There had never been any chemistry between them, but Stephan didn't know that. Gavin gave her a kiss on one cheek then stepped back and held her hands away from her sides to appreciate her transformation. "Wow. Look at you. You look good."

Nicole graced him with a huge smile. Gavin had always been kind to her. No legal request was too small. He was only in his late thirties, but he'd made a fortune by helping influential people find creative ways to interpret documents. He could have tried to use their acquaintance to facilitate a connection with the powerful men in her family, but he never had.

And that was why she trusted him.

"I thought it was time for a change," she said.

He held her hands a moment longer. "You were always beautiful, but now you're glowing. It's nice to see you smiling."

Nicole felt her face flush as she remembered exactly which comment had put that glow on her cheeks.

Stephan stepped closer, looking less than pleased at their conversation, "Stephan Andrade." Somehow he made his name sound like a threat. He slid a possessive hand onto the small of Nicole's back.

Gavin released Nicole to offer his hand to Stephan, "Gavin Burke. Before we start, I'd like to make it clear that I represent Nicole's interests. You might want to have your own people read the contract over before you sign it."

Stephan shook his hand, but Nicole could have sworn she saw Gavin wince when he did. Stephan said, "I have every intention of doing just that."

"It's probably also not a good idea for anyone outside of this office to know that your engagement isn't real," Gavin added.

In response to Stephan's look of displeasure, Nicole said, "I told Gavin the truth. I trust him."

"Apparently," Stephan said, not making an effort to hide his disapproval. His hand dropped from her back.

She and Gavin shared a quick look, the kind that makes you giggle in church. She bit her lip and shook her head. Stephan did take himself a bit too seriously, but nothing would be gained by annoying him to the point where he walked out without signing the paperwork.

Gavin led the way to a table where he had the paperwork laid out. After they were all seated, he said, "It's pretty cut and dried. This is essentially a pre-prenuptial. Read it over. Stephan you're agreeing that in the event of your engagement to Nicole ending, you will give her the right of first refusal at the same price that you purchased Corisi Ltd. You're also agreeing that for the extent of time that Corisi Ltd is owned by you, Nicole Corisi will be the acting CEO unless she resigns the position. Nicole, by signing this contract you are going forward with your father's initial acceptance of Stephan's buyout offer. The company and it's profits will be solely Stephan's until such a time that you either break off your engagement or you marry. Marriage will revert the company to a co-ownership status without the necessity of monetary exchange. Are the terms acceptable to you both?"

A knock at the door was followed by an apologetic secretary's stepping into the room for a moment, "Mr. Burke, I'm so sorry to interrupt, but there is a man here who is adamant that he see Miss Corisi immediately."

Who would come here?

Nicole held her breath the long moment it took the secretary to add, "He said his name is George Miles. I told him you were busy, but he insists that it's urgent."

Stephan spun back to Nicole and asked, "Miles…isn't he…."

Nicole nodded. "He's the Vice President of marketing at Corisi Ltd."

"Did you tell him why you're here?"

Nicole said, "No." Then she remembered something. "But I did tell Thomas."

Gavin didn't seem to mind the interruption at all. He said, "Send him in. This should be interesting."

George rushed into the office, his face was red and his forehead glistened with sweat as if he had taken the stairs. "Nicole. Is it too late? Did you sign anything yet?"

Nicole got up to meet him. "George, calm down." The last thing her month needed was another heart attack.

"Did you sign anything?"

"No, not yet, but I'm going to."

He wiped his forehead. "You don't have to." The glare he gave Stephan made his opinion of him clear to everyone in the room. "When Thomas told me what you were planning, I knew why you were doing it. You're afraid your brother is going to fire all of us when he takes over, and you think this is the only way you can stop him."

It is, Nicole thought.

"But it's not," George rushed to say. "I've invested well over the years. A few of the others have also. If we pool our resources and you take out a partial loan, we could buy Corisi Ltd outright."

Nicole whispered, "I can't take your money." It was a moot point anyway since the only purchaser the will would allow was Stephan.

"Then let Dominic run the company for a while. Even if he fires all of us, we'll be ok. You don't have to do *this*." And by this he clearly meant Stephan.

"I can't lose you, too." She hadn't meant to say it, but the truth poured out of her in a tone so full of desperation that the room instantly, painfully stilled. *Oh, God. Why did I say that?*

The older man's eyes shone with responding emotion. "Is that what this is about, Nicole? I've known you since you were five. My wife jokes that you are the out-of-marriage child I never had to pay support for. Do you think you won't be welcome at my house on the holidays because of anything your brother could do?"

That's exactly what I think.

Nicole fisted her hands and kept her thoughts to herself.

George stepped closer and laid a gentle hand on one of her stiff arms. "You don't have to prove anything to anyone. We know who you are and nothing and no one could change that. Come on. Come back to the office with me and we'll find another solution."

No.

Nicole searched Stephan's face for some hint of what he was thinking. She wasn't sure what she was hoping she'd see, but she was disappointed when she saw nothing.

In the beginning it had all been about saving the jobs of the people she'd known since childhood, but somehow it had become much more complicated than that. Was she a fool to hope that beneath Stephan's tough exterior he was still the man she remembered?

She was moved beyond words that George and the others had charged to her rescue. She'd never dared to hope that they could care for her the way she cared about them. She would never forget this day; the day she saw her first proof that some things could survive the Corisi curse.

If all of this was still only about saving the jobs of George and the others, she might have walked out that door and taken him up on his brainstorming offer. However, somewhere along the way, she'd let herself begin to hope again.

She couldn't walk away from Stephan and his family. Not yet. If she did, there was a good chance she'd never see any of them again. Seven years ago, she'd run back to her father's house and accepted the loss as inevitable. This time she wasn't willing to leave so easily, and right now the fake engagement was the only thing holding them together.

I'm not afraid of the fight anymore.

The old her would have chosen to play it safe. She would have gone along with her father's will and thought there was nothing she could do about it. She would have accepted the superficial intimacy Stephan had offered her and expected him to leave her.

Not anymore.

If she lost her inheritance, it wouldn't be because she hadn't fought for it.

And if she and Stephan separated at the end of this fake engagement, she was going to walk away knowing that she had been brave enough to keep her heart open, and strong enough to demand to be treated with respect.

Her decision was made.

Nicole hugged George and said, "I love you for coming here today, George. I'll never forget that you did this for me, but I'm here because I want to be. Stephan and I fell in love back when I worked for his father, and we've been secretly seeing each other for a while now." She walked over and took Stephan's hand, smiling up at him to prove to George that there was nothing lascivious going on. "I want to marry Stephan. I love him. Please, try to be happy for me."

Stephan pulled her into his side and she could hear his heart beating wildly in his chest.

George looked back and forth between them, not quite sure he was willing to believe her. "You're sure?"

Nicole wrapped both arms around Stephan's middle and rested her check on his chest. "I'm sure. Go back and tell everyone that we'll invite them to our engagement party when we have one, so they can celebrate with us."

Gavin led George back out the door.

George stopped just before he walked out the door and said, "Hurt her, Stephan, and it will be the last thing you do."

STEPHAN CONTINUED TO hold Nicole against him. He felt like he'd been run over by a mack truck and dragged down a highway.

She loves me?

No, she couldn't. Their engagement was purely a business arrangement. She'd made that abundantly clear to him last night.

It was all a lie. He knew it. So, why had he stopped breathing and felt a little woozy when she'd claimed that she really wanted to marry him?

Without looking down at her, he forced out a question he wasn't sure he wanted to hear the answer to. "Do you love me, Nicole?"

Nicole stepped out of his embrace and he felt both relieved and profoundly disappointed at the same time. She said, "I had to say something. I couldn't let him leave here worrying about me." She walked over to the table and signed the paperwork.

Gavin had returned and was watching the two of them closely.

Stephan strode over and signed the contract.

"It's done," Nicole said. "Thank you, Gavin. I'll be in touch." She shook his hand and gave him a light kiss on one cheek. She turned to Stephan and said, "I'll see you at home."

Stephan's stomach did a painful flip.

Without another word, Nicole turned and walked out of the office. He simply stood there, watching her go.

Gavin said, "You don't deserve her."

Four truer words had never been spoken.

"Just send a copy of the papers over to my office," Stephan said and strode out.

Mr. Smooth Lawyer might be in love with Nicole. He might even be close enough to her that she shared confidences with him, but she wasn't going home with *him*.

Nicole was already gone by the time he reached the street. He wanted to chase her down, demand that she tell him the real reason she had fought so hard for her father's company, and kiss her till they both forgot why they didn't belong together.

Instead, he headed to Tiffany's and bought her the biggest, most expensive diamond they had.

CHAPTER *Eleven*

WHO KNEW BURNING sauce could make so much smoke? Nicole coughed and waved a hand towel in front of the smoke detector as it went off for the second time. Even in shorts and a white t-shirt, she was working herself up into a sweat.

Tonight she was celebrating. She'd done it! The top executives at her father's company—no, now it was just Corisi Ltd—could rest easy. Their jobs were safe. Her quasi family unit would not be dismantled, at least not in the immediate future. And her phone would finally stop ringing with calls from a brother she refused to talk to.

With that stress behind her, Nicole was free to focus her attention on an equally pressing matter—Stephan. How did you say thank you to a man who purchased a computer software company for you? She knew how his family would.

Confident that she'd found the perfect gesture, Nicole had written her first grocery list and had happily, successfully purchased all of the items for the meal at the local supermarket. What she hadn't anticipated was how quickly the heat from the oven would overtake the effects of the air conditioner.

The oven. *The chicken!*

Opening the oven door revealed a now blackened-beyond-recognition main entrée that billowed thick smoke into Nicole's face. Her eyes stung and began to water.

"Corisi family recipe?" Stephan asked over the smoke alarm.

Nicole spun from peering into the oven. Stephan was leaning against one side of the door frame, jacket flung across his shoulder.

"Very funny," Nicole snapped and waved a hand in front of her face in an ineffective attempt to dissipate the smoke. "How do you get the oven to stop smoking?"

Stephan laid his jacket on the back of one of the chairs in the kitchen and walked over to where she was. She didn't move. He came to a close stop. His head came down until their lips were almost touching. At first Nicole thought he was going to try to kiss her again, but instead he reached behind her and turned a couple of the stove's dials. "It helps if you turn it off," he murmured.

Nicole tried to back up, but her legs were already against the stove. Leaning back brought her rump in contact with his hand briefly. She jumped forward as if burned, only to find that doing so pressed her chest against his. His quickly indrawn breath revealed that their fleeting physical contact had affected him as much as it had her.

She slid sideways and escaped to a few feet away, cursing herself for not changing into something nicer before he came home. Nothing was turning out the way she'd planned it. "The internet said that chicken and pasta is one of the easiest meals to make." She blew a stray hair out of her face. "They are full of shit."

His chuckle was unexpected, and the best sound she'd heard in a long time. "I have a full-time cook, Nicole."

"I know," she said defensively. "I wanted to do something special to thank you for helping me today."

He studied her for another moment, as if he'd been about to say something but had decided against it, and said, "Maddy would love this story. Her rule was that if she cooked for you, you had to eat it. The whole family was relieved when she married a chef. Before Richard, we were considering buying stock in an antacid company."

Despite the fact that everything she'd planned for the evening had gone impossibly wrong, she smiled at the mention of his little spitfire of a cousin. "How could she not know how to cook with Elise and Katrine around? They are amazing."

"I don't know if you've noticed, but Maddy doesn't take advice well. She does what she wants to do...even with recipes." Stephan shuddered.

"I really like Maddy," Nicole said spontaneously.

Stephan looked like he was engaged in some inner debate. Finally, he said, "I believe you mean that."

Nicole leaned back against a corner of the counter. "Your family has always been kind to me, Stephan. When our engagement ends, I'll make sure that it's done in a way that makes you look good in the eye of the public. I would never deliberately do anything to harm your family."

Her words had the opposite effect on Stephan than she'd anticipated. His face tightened and he said, "Planning the end already? Do you regret signing the paperwork?"

"No, do you?"

Instead of answering, Stephan tossed Nicole a small box. She caught it just in time. Opening it revealed a 24-carat emerald-cut diamond in a raised platinum setting. Elegant, and wildly expensive. It was exactly the kind of ring you'd expect a Corisi to want. Nicole's heart sank. She took it out of the velvet box and turned it slowly between her fingers.

Not me at all.

"You don't like it," Stephan stated flatly.

Nicole grimaced. "It's fine."

He said gruffly, "You can take it back and get something you want."

What she wanted was not something she was going to find in a jewelry case at Tiffany's. His choice of ring for her made it painfully obvious that he did not know her. She slid the large diamond on her left finger. "It's beautiful, Stephan, and it's only for a short time anyway. Thank you."

He let out a harsh breath. "Most women would love that ring."

Nicole bristled, "I said it was beautiful."

His frustration was growing. "I spent thirty...actually *thirty-five* million dollars on you today. Thirty-five million dollars. Do you know any other women who can say they've had that kind of day? And you don't look happy. I thought you'd be grateful."

"I am. I cooked-" Sudden comprehension hit her. "Do you mean grateful? Or *grateful?*"

He put both hands up in mock defense. "I…"

She jabbed one finger into his chest and said, "Let's get a few points straight right now. This is a business arrangement. Your help bought you the rights to one conversion patent. That's it. And although you did spend a lot of money today, you'll get it all back in a few weeks."

107

She waved her left ring finger in front of his face. "Along with this. I hope you kept the receipt. I meant what I said last night. *I don't know if I like you.* You're rude. You're arrogant. Just because you're gorgeous, doesn't mean every woman wants to have sex with you. Women want more than hot suggestions whispered into their ears. They want conversation. They want…" His amused expression halted her tirade. Hands on her hips, she said, "What? What are you thinking? Just say it."

A devil of mischief sparkled in those beautiful blue eyes. "No, go on. I'm listening." When she didn't, he prompted, "You were telling me what women want."

She shook her head and said, "I'm serious."

He smiled.

"You're an ass," she said.

His smile widened, but he stepped closer. "But I'm a gorgeous ass."

She threw an oven mitt at him when he reached for her. "Don't touch me."

He didn't, but he continued to stand so close to her that her body began to betray her. She licked her suddenly dry lips. He leaned an inch closer. "So, no whispering ideas into your ear? No touching? Just conversation? That's what you want?" His lips were so close she could almost taste him.

She gulped, "Yes."

"Because you want to sleep, every night, all alone in your little twin-bed?"

No. "Yes," she forced the words out, trying to ignore how her skin tingled with anticipation of his touch—how her body was clenching, moistening, preparing for what she was refusing.

"Do you know what I want?" he asked, his voice practically purring.

Oh, God.

He stepped back and said, "Pizza, because I don't think I can eat that chicken. Do you mind ordering some while I make a few phone calls?" He sauntered over to pick up his jacket again and added, "I'll be in the living room, since I don't have an office anymore. Then we can eat and *talk*." He emphasized the last word and her scowl gained a deep laugh from him. "Unless you have another suggestion?"

Not one that didn't include smacking that smug look off his face.

He swung the jacket over one shoulder and headed for the door. "Oh, and ask them to put the ham and pineapple on only half. Fruit doesn't belong on pizza."

As soon as he was out of sight, Nicole plopped down onto one of the chairs.

He remembered my favorite toppings.

Would she ever figure him out?

CHAPTER *Twelve*

FOR THE NEXT few days, Stephan and Nicole talked. They met at the small table in his kitchen each morning at seven thirty. His cook made them both light fare and coffee. He asked her about her plans for the day and then shared his. They took the elevator down to the lobby together, awkwardly parting with a wave that seemed to amuse him.

They met again for dinner in his ultra modern dining room. At first they had contained their conversations to work anecdotes, but as the rapport between them became more comfortable, their topics expanded. Nicole shared with Stephan her concern over meeting some resistance as she took over the CEO position at Corisi Ltd. She hadn't expected to have to defend herself to the same people who would have been fired had she not fought for them. Stephan listened to all of her concerns and then suggested some ways to unruffle their feathers. His suggestions worked, which increased the fragile trust that was building between them.

Mid-way through one evening meal, Nicole said, "Your mother called. The party for your new nephew is on Saturday."

"What did you say?"

"I said we would go."

"I wish you'd talked to me about this first."

A sickening realization. "You don't want me around your family."

"Nicole…"

"Don't *Nicole* me. Say what you mean. Do you think they won't like me? Your mother actually asked me to go early so she could teach me some recipes."

"My family loves you and that's the problem."

"I already told you that when the time comes…"

He ran a frustrated hand through his blond hair, "Don't you get it? Every time you talk to them it's a lie. They don't know that none of this is real. I'm not going to let you hurt my family more than you…"

Nicole stood up and threw her napkin on the table. "Finish that sentence, Stephan. No, wait, I'll finish it for you. You won't let me hurt them more than I already have. You still blame me for what Dominic did to your father. I thought we were becoming friends if nothing else. I thought you understood that I would have done anything for your family if I could have." An angry tear ran down her cheek. "You don't want me around your family? You tell them. You explain why I didn't want to go to a party to celebrate a baby that I helped come into this world."

With that, Nicole crossed through the living room and slammed the door of her bedroom.

STEPHAN SLAMMED A fist down onto the table.

Great. Now she's crying.

That woman was impossible.

This was supposed to be entertaining and temporary, a way to finally get her out of his system. He wasn't supposed to rush through a shower each morning, just so he'd have a few more minutes of her company before he went off to work. In the middle of meetings, his thoughts shouldn't fill with images of her, and what she was doing at her own company that day. And never had he imagined that he would leave unfinished projects on his desk just so he could be home in time to have dinner with her.

He was following after her, hanging on her every word like some besotted fool—but was that enough for her?

No.

She wanted everything.

When had he completely lost control of this situation?

He didn't want her around his family, and he was right to protect them from her. The more time they spent with her, the more they would be hurt when she left.

At the end of the day, she was still a Corisi.

He knew that, but the scene from the meeting with her lawyer haunted him. There had been real fear in her voice and he didn't want to acknowledge it, because it implied something that was becoming difficult to ignore.

Nicole was not like her brother.

She couldn't be and still inspire the kind of loyalty the men at her father's company had shown her. The woman he'd tried to define her as would not have delivered his cousin's baby, and she wouldn't have won over his family.

Indecision and regret were not luxuries he normally allowed himself, but the questions kept coming. What if he was wrong? And what was it about being with Nicole that made it difficult for him to look at himself in the mirror?

She couldn't be as genuine and caring as she pretended to be, because if she was—then he was an ass. A complete and unsalvageable ass.

Now was not the time to start second-guessing all of his decisions. He'd set himself on a course from which there was no turning back. By now, Dominic's software was the digital equivalent of swiss cheese. All Stephan had to do was wait, and everything would fall into place. When his servers proved worthless, Dominic would crumble beneath a deadly financial hit, allowing Stephan to step in and not only take back his family's island, but also profit immeasurably as China turned to him for a solution.

Everything he had been working for was finally within his grasp.

He wasn't going to apologize to Nicole, but nor was he going to block her from seeing his family this time.

This one time.

After that, the less they were together, the better it would be for all of them.

CHAPTER *Thirteen*

ON FRIDAY MORNING, Nicole wondered if saying yes to Maddy had been such a good idea. Stephan was out of the office for the day, dealing with some distribution issue in Connecticut, so Maddy had asked Nicole to swing by his office for her, and pick up some tickets she'd left there. "No need to bother Stephan," she'd said. Maddy remembered exactly where she'd left them.

The temp secretary guarding Stephan's office had hesitated to admit Nicole, but one flash of the enormous emerald-cut diamond on her left finger had changed her mind.

This feels wrong.

She hadn't paid much attention to his desk during her last visit, but it was an impressive piece of furniture. High-tech beyond what even her father had owned. Glass and gray metal with an embedded touch screen. It no doubt had other features whose functions would only be apparent when activated. *Nice.*

114

The files on Stephan's computer were likely encrypted, but the metal drawers beneath the desk opened easily. Maddy had asked Stephan to hold onto her tickets to an upcoming art show. The top drawer revealed nothing of importance.

While rifling through the middle drawer, Nicole found something that made her legs give way beneath her, dropping her into Stephan's chair. It was a photo of her and Stephan, taken by a roving park photographer the day of their one and only date. She'd forgotten this picture even existed. His hair was longer, his dress was casual. They were looking at each other and smiling like the future was theirs.

She *hadn't* imagined his feelings for her; they were evident in the way he was looking at her in the photo. No matter what had come later, his feelings had been real for her that day.

Beneath that picture was an invitation to a fundraiser in California. One week from that day. Scribbled across the formal invite was a personal note in masculine writing. *We're taking bets on if this is the year you'll break down and come. Kayla says you should get your butt out here before our kids start having kids. Mark.*

There was a small photo attached with a paperclip. Stephan's old west coast friends. They sounded sincere and successful, not at all how his father had described them. Not the outrageously successful level that her family fought for, but the comfortable middle class, two car, one boat, family vacation kind of comfortable.

And they looked happy. So much happier than she could ever remember being.

Nicole stuffed both photos and the invitation in her purse. There were no tickets in any of Stephan's drawers.

115

Maddy must have wanted me to find the photos. Why would Stephan keep a photo of our date in his desk?

Was it possible that he still had feelings for her?

Did she dare let herself believe?

WITH STEPHAN'S GRUDGING permission, Nicole went early on Saturday to help Katrine and Elise cook. She was wrapped in an apron, elbow deep in "gravy" when Maddy entered the kitchen with her new baby in her arms.

The food was temporarily forgotten.

"Nicole!" Maddy exclaimed and handed Joseph to her mother so she could give Nicole a hug. The Andrades were quickly breaking down Nicole's personal-space inhibitions. Nicole returned the tight hug.

The four women took a few moments to coo over the little one in their presence.

"Did you go to Stephan's office for me?" Maddy asked. Instantly, Katrine and Elise spun to look at Nicole.

Like they knew. Like they knew everything. Nicole nodded slowly, unsure of what to say.

Katrine asked, "Did you find the photo?"

Nicole went beet red. "You know about the photo? Do you know…"

Elise laughed, "Nicole, we know about the whole thing. My daughter can't keep a secret. Not even her own. Do you have it with you?"

Nicole dug the picture out of her purse and shared it with the group.

Katrine shook her head sadly, "That's probably the last time I saw that expression on Stephan's face. He used to be so happy. He still smiles, but not from the heart. Not like this."

116

Elise took the photo and studied it. "Maddy, usually I tell you how wrong you are when you interfere, but look at their faces. I see why you had to do something."

Maddy shrugged while admitting, "I thought so, but now I don't know. They both look miserable today."

Nicole said, "You know that I'm still here, right?"

Maddy smiled sheepishly. "Sorry. But you do. I thought you'd be halfway to a real proposal by now."

Reaching behind her to untie her apron, Nicole slipped it over her head and off. "Even if what we felt that day was real, how could it survive what came afterwards? How could anything?"

"You still love my son. It'll work out," Katrine assured her.

Nicole shook head and tears thickened her voice. "No, I loved the man who thought he could save the world one silly documentary at a time. I loved how good and honest he was. And I loved who I was when he looked at me. He doesn't look at me like that anymore. He doesn't even want me around you after today."

Elise walked over with her grandchild snuggled to her chest and said something fast and cutting in Italian.

Katrine said, "I worry about Stephan. He was always so idealistic. There was never a gray area for him. He changed when Victor sold the company to your brother. Stephan blamed himself and you. He walked away from everything he cared about, and became someone he thought we needed him to be. I used to be able to get him to open up to me when he was younger, but he's closed himself off from all of us. I just want to shake him and tell him that he doesn't have to be this man, this stranger. He's in a bad place right now, Nicole, because he feels like he just lost to your brother a second time. Call it mother's intuition; something happened in China that he won't discuss. He needs you back in his life. You might be the only one who can reach him before he goes too far."

Nicole wiped away the tears that started spilling down her cheeks. "I don't think I can. I'm not sure the man I love is even in there anymore."

Maddy said, "He is and this will all work out."

Oh, Maddy.

Did we even grow up on the same planet?

Nicole snapped, "That sounds nice, but it's not reality. Happy endings are a lie we tell our children to believe in, a cruel lie. In the end, most of us just fall into bed alone, relieved to have survived the day. I am just beginning to figure out what I need to be happy. How can I possibly help Stephan?"

Katrine put both arms around her shoulders and simply hugged her. In the safety of her embrace, Nicole allowed herself to cry out the emotions she'd tried so hard to hold in. She cried for the father who had never loved her, the mother she had lost so long ago, and the brother who she loved as much as she hated. She cried for a man who had lost himself on his way to save the world. And she clung to the woman who kept murmuring that it would all somehow be ok.

Elise brought her a tissue when she settled down and she blew her nose loudly.

Maddy started to say something, but Katrine raised her hand and silenced her. After a moment, Katrine said, "You've been through so much, Nicole. It's probably wrong of me to ask you to risk getting hurt more, but I see the way my son looks at you. You're right, though—the easy, happily ever after kind of love is a myth. Love is more than that. It's a decision to care about someone even when you want to strangle them and to forgive them for not being perfect. Love is hard work. It involves real risk and sometimes real loss. But if you don't let yourself believe in the person you love, then you miss out on the good in them and the chance to have a real partner in life. I can't guarantee you that if you give my son a chance that he will deserve it, but I know he cares about you. I know that you're the kind of woman who could bring him back to us."

Elise leaned in to add, "Whatever you decide, we'll understand."

Impulsively, Nicole pulled the invitation out of her purse. "I found this with the photo. It's an invitation to a fundraiser in California. I think Stephan wants to go."

They passed the invitation around.

"You're right. He kept that invitation for a reason," Maddy said.

Katrine agreed and added, "He should go. You should both go. Being around his old friends might help him remember what was important to him."

If only it were that easy. "I don't think Stephan will say yes if I ask him."

Elise said, "Then don't *just* ask him."

Nicole said, "I'm sorry?"

The women exchanged a quick look.

Elise said, "Maddy, go stir the sauce while Katrine and I explain men to Nicole."

Nicole watched her walk away with some trepidation.

Maddy laughed from across the room. "You *should* be scared, Nicole. They gave me the same talk when I got married. I'm still scarred."

Katrine motioned for them to sit at the counter of the kitchen island. "Just watch the food, Maddy. Now, Nicole, some of what we're going to tell you will sound crazy to you at first, but women have been using these techniques since the beginning of time. When you're dealing with something important like this, and you know your man is going to be difficult to convince, you can take advantage of his biological weaknesses."

Bemused, Nicole shook her head. "I have no idea what you're talking about."

Elise pulled her chair closer and said, "Step one is called: The Shake Up. It's all about getting his attention and keeping it."

Alessandro stuck his head into the kitchen and said, "How is everything?"

Elise scooted him out. "We're cooking, Alessandro. Go talk to the men."

He looked around, "But.."

"Out," Elise said after her husband left reluctantly. "Ok, where were we?"

Katrine said, "You were still on step one."

"I don't know if I feel comfortable with this," Nicole said.

Katrine nodded sympathetically but stressed, "Nicole, the Andrades are loyal and loving, but they can also be stubborn and bossy. You've got to know how to maneuver around their egos."

Elise added, "It's really for their own good. Everyone ends up happy, and they are none the wiser."

Nicole said, "I'd rather just be honest with Stephan. I'll tell him how important it is to both of us that we go."

Elise and Katrine shook their heads. Maddy chuckled while stirring the sauce.

With a clear look of skepticism on her face, Elise said, "You can try it, if you think it will work."

Imagining the scenario in her head, Nicole had to concede that it probably wouldn't. So far reasoning with Stephan had not gotten her very far. What if going to California held the answers to all of her questions? Wasn't it worth a little subterfuge? "Ok, I'm in. What is step one?"

Maddy piped in from across the room, "Just remember that I warned you."

Elise shushed her with a wave of her hand. "The male physiology…"

Maddy cut in, "La la la, I can't hear this again."

Katrine said, "Elise, maybe you should skip that part. I'm sure Nicole doesn't need the birds and the bees talk."

Shrugging, Elise moved on. "Then back to the actual steps. Tomorrow, when Stephan comes home from work, this is what you should do…"

On the way home from the party, Stephan was pensive. He sat next to her in the back of the limo, but they were about halfway home before he said anything.

"My family really likes you."

Did he have to look so miserable about that fact? "I really like them."

He turned away from her, looking out the window while speaking to her. "In the future, we'll make some excuse why you can't accept their invitations. I haven't changed my mind. I don't want you spending any time with them, Nicole. There is no reason to involve them in this."

"I understand," Nicole said.

They couldn't be more involved, she thought, biting the inside of her check to stop herself from smiling.

"So, it's settled." He sounded relieved and surprised.

"Yes," she said.

If by settled, you mean that this conversation just convinced me that you deserve every moment of what you'll be coming home to tomorrow.

CHAPTER *Fourteen*

NICOLE FELT A bit ridiculous walking around the house in a little red bikini, waiting for Stephan to come home from work. When she heard the click of the outside door, she sprinted to the lounge chair she'd placed on the patio and pretended to be sunbathing.

He walked out onto the balcony.

She pretended she didn't notice his arrival. Then she said casually, "Oh, Stephan, you're back."

The expression on his face was almost comical. *It couldn't really be this easy. Could it?*

Step One: The Shake Up. Elise assured her that this step was a breeze because bikinis muddle men's minds. Until now, Nicole hadn't actually believed her. Lean in all asset areas, Nicole had never considered her figure particularly sexy. Yet, when she stood slowly, Stephan's eyes popped and his jaw went slack.

This might actually be fun.

"How was work?" she tried to sound casual.

He didn't answer at first, which gave her the confidence to continue. She arched her back, as if stretching after a long rest, enjoying the impact her moves were having on him. So this was why women invested in push up bras and sexy outfits. Knowing that looking at her was wreaking havoc with Stephan's ability to think was a powerful turn-on.

The men in her past made sense to her now. She'd been passive and insecure, grateful for whatever affection they had given her, and devastated when they'd left her.

No surprise that they hadn't cherished her when she hadn't valued herself.

Her passive acceptance of loss had also cost her Stephan. She saw that now. Yes, she had gone to Dominic and asked him to stop, but she had accepted Dominic's decision without a fight. She'd accepted her brother's indifference toward her feelings as she had always accepted it from her father, convinced that there was no way she could win against either Corisi.

But she *had* won.

By signing the company over to Stephan, she'd finally beaten both her father and her brother. She wasn't a flower in a thorn bush anymore. She didn't need rescuing.

She was free.

She was strong.

And this time she was going to fight for Stephan.

Right now, that meant getting him out to California, even if it was the last place he thought he wanted to be. The strategy to do it was simple enough, but it was difficult to concentrate when his eyes were lit with desire for her. She was basking in the heat that was spreading through her body in response.

"Stephan?"

"Huh?"

"Are you listening to me?"

His face reddened just a tad and he shook his head as if to clear it.

She stepped closer to him, enjoying the way his eyes widened with pleasure at her advance, the way he seemed to stop breathing. The sizzle between them was…*delicious.*

His hand reached for her waist and stopped. "Are you changing the rules, Nicole?"

She retreated a step. "No, I just wanted to ask you a question, but I can put something on if this bothers you."

"No," he said automatically but then, sounding a bit more strangled, he added, "Yes. Maybe you should."

Nicole turned and bent to pick up her cover up from the floor where she'd laid it earlier. She almost let out a nervous giggle as she slid it on one shoulder at a time. A reverse strip tease. She was so far outside her comfort zone that she would not have been surprised if she had heard Stephan start laughing.

When she glanced back at him, he made no effort to conceal exactly how her antics were affecting him. From the desire in his eyes, to the bulge in his pants, there was no denying that she had woken the tiger within him.

Other men had wanted to have sex with her, but none had *burned* for her. None had ignited a responding need within her, one so strong she was quickly losing her own ability to focus on anything but how he made her feel. The younger her had once yearned to have his lips pressed against hers. The mature woman she'd become hungered for that and so much more.

Focus. This is about California, not ripping his clothes off.

Not yet.

125

She almost lost her nerve and stopped the game, but she quickly reminded herself of how much was at stake. Somewhere beneath all of his bravado and sarcasm, was a man who'd kept her picture with him all these years. To save his family, he'd turned his back on his own dreams and her. No wonder he didn't trust her. For now, he only offered sex, but if she could help him remember who he'd once been, maybe they could finish this journey – together.

Taking a deep breath, Nicole walked back over to him and initiated Step Two: The Request. Expect a refusal.

"Maddy found an invitation in your desk to a weekend fundraising event off Seal Beach, California. We should go."

"No," he said without hesitation in a tone that implied there was no room for negotiation.

"It sounds like a worthwhile cause: a boat race to raise money to help clean up the beaches."

"No, and you can tell Maddy that she is not going to be working for me long if she keeps looking in my desk. Forget it, I'll tell her."

So much for the direct approach working.

She could stop now and accept that he clearly didn't want this trip. She might even be able to keep their relationship platonic until the dissolution of their engagement and save herself from further heartbreak. The pivotal decision she needed to make right here and now was if she believed in Stephan. Not a perfect Stephan. Not a fantasy Stephan. Did she believe that beneath all of his anger there was still a good man with whom she could imagine spending the rest of her life?

Yes.

Then her course was set.

Love is a risk I'm willing to take.

126

California, here we come.

Step Three: The Undesirable Alternative. Make it count.

Nicole did her best sashay across the penthouse to get a glass of water from the kitchen. Stephan followed. Her deliberate stretch for a glass from one of the top shelves earned a delightful, tormented male groan. *Good.* Success relied on not giving him too much time to think through his options.

Turning so that she rested one hip against the counter, Nicole poured water into her glass with a slightly unsteady hand. "Ok, well, then you should probably call your mother. She asked me to come over and start planning the wedding with her and Elise, but I told her I couldn't because we were going to be in California."

He ran a frustrated hand through his hair. "We're not even getting married. What the hell is there to plan for?"

One lie led to another. "She doesn't know that, and she's excited."

The scowl on his face had been accurately predicted.

Damn, those Andrade women were good. They could have scripted this exchange.

Step Four – His Decision. It is essential to maintain a straight face while he works out the solution.

Nicole clasped her hands in front of her and did her best to appear sincerely worried. "Should I call her back and tell her that we'll be here?"

Stephan crossed the room and didn't stop until she was backed against the counter. He leaned forward, placing one hand on either side of the counter behind her, trapping her. Ok, that wasn't the anticipated response. He was supposed to reluctantly agree.

There was no Step Five – nothing that covered this contingency.

"I get the feeling that you're playing with me," he said, practically purring the words into her ear.

Nicole made the mistake of looking up into his sky blue eyes. The desire she saw in them seared through her. She licked her lips nervously.

He ran a thumb softly across her moist bottom lip. Nicole caught her breath.

"Why do you want to go to California, Nicole? What's in it for you?"

"I don't know what you're talking about."

With just that one thumb, he traced the line of her jaw then his hand moved slowly, purposefully, to the sensitive skin behind her ear and buried it in her thick hair. "Yes, you do. You are not a very good liar." His hand cupped the back of her head. "Are you beginning to regret your ground rules?"

Rules? Nicole could barely remember her name when he touched her.

Would it be so wrong to give in to something they both wanted?

If by doing so, I lose the chance of something more meaningful, then yes.

I can't give up now.

Step Five – The Truth?

"I do want to be with you, Stephan, but…"

His jaw clenched while he waited for her to finish.

"But not here. Not like this." She waved her hand to indicate that she meant more than his penthouse.

He studied her expression for a moment before saying, "A different location won't change who we are."

Nicole laid one hand on top of his on the counter and said, "This might be all we ever have. A few weeks from now, we could be out of each other's lives for good. All I'm asking you for is one weekend. I don't want to think about your family or my family. I want a weekend with you. Just you."

"Why California? We could go anywhere."

Please just say yes. This could be our last chance. Nicole kept her tone casual. "A sailboat fundraiser sounds like fun. I want to do something spontaneous and crazy. Don't you? When was the last time you did something just because it was fun?"

"One weekend. No strings? No promises?" He looked skeptical.

"Yes," she said huskily.

"You could accept that?" His blue eyes were dark with emotion.

I hope I don't have to. I hope your family is right. Nicole nodded.

He withdrew both hands and stepped away from her. "We'll fly out Friday night."

He said yes.

I can't believe he said yes to a weekend away with his old friends.

And I said yes to sleeping with him.

Oh, God.

By next Monday things were either going to be better or so much worse.

CHAPTER *Fifteen*

A TALL, THIN man in jeans and a light blue buttoned down shirt stepped away from his hybrid car and met Stephan and Nicole on the tarmac of a small private airfield as they descended the stairs from Stephan's jet into the warm Californian sunshine. He gave Stephan a back thumping hug. "Stephan, it's good to see you!"

Stephan returned his hug, but appeared somewhat uneasy. He looked around and said, "I'd hired a car for the weekend."

"Did you think I wouldn't meet you?" His friend asked with a smile and added, "You don't send a car to pick up family…even when they ignore your phone messages." The jab was good-natured.

"I've been busy," Stephan said, sounding the closest to apologetic that Nicole had ever heard him.

The man looked past Stephan and smiled at Nicole. He offered her his hand and said, "Mark Allen. You must be the infamous Nicole. I've heard a lot about you. A lot. "

Nicole shook his hand warmly, instantly liking him. "Really?"

Stephan took their two carry on bags from the pilot. He said, "Don't be an ass, Mark."

Mark opened the trunk of his mid-sized vehicle and winked at Nicole. "He's always been defensive when it comes to you. If he doesn't want me to say anything, he shouldn't get so upset when I do. I can't help myself."

Stephan threw their bags into the trunk and closed it. "This is why you got punched out by that football player Freshman year. You don't know when to stop."

Looking back and forth between the two men, Nicole did not see any family resemblance. She asked, "Are you actually related?"

Mark shook his head as he moved to open the front passenger door and motioned for Nicole to get in. "Feels like it, though. We met when he came out here for college, but it's been a long time since we've seen him." He arched an eyebrow when he looked back at Stephan. "Too long."

Stephan ignored the jab and folded his large frame into the back seat.

Nicole settled into her seat, but hopped up when she felt something. Reaching beneath her, she pulled out a Lego spaceship.

After getting in and closing his door, Mark said, "Oh, sorry, put it in here." He opened the center compartment. She did. "I swear toys multiply. It doesn't matter how many you take out of the car, there are always more." He studied her for a moment.

Nicole had dressed casually for the trip, following Stephan's lead. There was something incredibly freeing about not worrying about being perfectly manicured every moment of the day.

Mark asked, "Different from what you're used to?"

Nicole adjusted the strap across her shoulder and said, "Yes, but in a good way."

As Mark started the car, Stephan said, "We're staying at the…"

"No," Mark countered. "Maddy canceled that reservation after I spoke with her. We haven't seen you in years, the kids are excited to meet the mysterious man who sends them presents, and Kayla aired out the guest room for you."

Stephan leaned forward between the seats, his tone firm, "That's nice, but Nicole would probably be more comfortable in the hotel."

Sure, blame me. Nicole crossed her jean clad legs and smiled sweetly at Stephan. "I'm ok with staying with your friends."

Stephan sat back with a frustrated growl.

Mark laughed. "You've got the rest of your lives to chase each other around hotel rooms. You're only here for two days. You're coming home with us."

The topic was closed for further debate.

Nicole wanted to turn in her seat to see Stephan's expression, but she didn't. She was too busy trying to figure out how she felt about the change in plans. On one hand, she couldn't have hoped for more than the warm welcome Stephan's friends had extended to both of them. On the other hand, she sympathized with the lack of enthusiasm emanating from Stephan. The promise of a steamy weekend getaway was disappearing as quickly as the airport behind them.

Mark checked in on his friend with his rearview mirror. "Ah, the angst of new love. You'll live Stephan."

Stephan threatened, "Payback will come tomorrow when I run your new boat into a sandbar."

Unimpressed by the threat, Mark included Nicole in his joke. "He says that like it wouldn't happen anyway. Luckily, he can afford to replace it. How many things did you borrow and break when you used to stay with us in Palo Alto?"

"Everything you bought was old," Stephan said in amused defense.

"Yeah, because Kayla was on a save-the-world-through-extreme-recycling kick. It took a while to convince her that some new things might be easier on the environment." Mark shrugged. "At least my sailboat is new."

"I saw pictures of it online. Fifty footer, right? It looked sweet," Stephan said.

"It is. I had to promise Kayla I'd host a fundraiser every year that I own it. My boat isn't fast, but I lose every race in style."

Stephan chuckled, then said, "You've never asked me for a donation, Mark. You know I don't mind."

Mark said, "We're grateful that you've always supported our causes, Stephan, but we'd rather see you. I thought for sure this was another year that you'd ignore the invitation."

Stephan said, "I…"

Mark interrupted, "You don't have to explain. We're just glad you're here."

So am I. Nicole thought as she listened to the two men. Stephan looked years younger when his face relaxed and he laughed with his old friend. *This might actually work.*

I could get used to this.

Sitting on a wooden Adirondack chair on the back deck of the Allen home, Nicole took a moment to appreciate her surroundings. The house was middle class utopia – a four bedroom raised ranch, two baths, inground pool on a two-acre lot. Upon arrival, as if on cue, a yellow Labrador had bounded around the corner of the house to greet them with a tennis ball in his mouth. A moment later, two children – a boy and girl also came running from the backyard, Kyle and Kara – eight year old twins.

Heaven.

Kayla, Mark's wife, joined everyone on the front lawn a moment later. She completed the postcard perfect family. Like her husband, she was casually dressed — jeans, t-shirt, sandals. She appeared effortlessly confident, comfortable, and successful. The couple was well known both in California and in Washington, but you'd never guess it from their modest lifestyle. Kayla hugged Stephan like a long lost brother, then turned to give Nicole a warm welcome. After introducing the children, she'd herded everyone into the house. Once inside, Nicole had stepped out onto the back patio while Stephan and Mark discussed his new boat.

"Ask her," a young voice prompted.

"No, you ask her," another answered.

Kyle gave his sister a push in Nicole's direction. Nicole hid her grin. The two were adorable. Brown hair, brown eyes and so serious it was almost comical. "What do you want to know?"

Kara stepped forward and asked, "Is it true that you and Uncle Stephan are uber-rich?"

That wasn't a question Nicole had a ready answer for. "Why?"

Kyle said, "It's for her stupid website. She interviews everyone she meets. Don't let her take pictures of you. She'll post them with captions you won't like. Trust me."

Kara folded her arms and glared at her brother, "He's just jealous because people read *my* blog."

"You have a blog?" Nicole didn't mean to let so much of her surprise show. When did children become so tech savvy?

"Sure. Change a mind, change the world," she chimed. She settled down on a chair next to Nicole. "So, are you? Rich, I mean. My post needs a good angle."

Maybe coming onto the patio was a mistake. Nicole said, "Are your parents ok with this?"

Kara nodded. "Sure, Mom was going to interview you for her blog, but she told Dad that you don't do anything worth mentioning."

Ouch.

Kyle jumped in, "Kara, that's rude."

Kara quickly added, "It's not rude, it's true. Mom writes about people who raise money for charities or lobby for environmental causes. Do you do any of that, Nicole?"

"No," Nicole admitted reluctantly.

"See," Kara said. "So, can I interview you?"

Nicole hedged. "Let's talk more about it tomorrow."

Kyle smirked. "That's a no."

Kara said, "Get lost, Kyle."

Kyle opened the screen door to go back into the house. "Remember what I said about the pictures, Nicole."

Nicole laughed, "I will."

Kara flounced in her chair. "Mom says I have to love him because he's my brother. Do you have a brother, Nicole?"

"Yes," Nicole said. Suddenly serious.

"No. You can't be related to…Is your brother Dominic Corisi?" Kara practically leapt out of her seat with a squeal.

Grudgingly, Nicole said, "Yes."

Kara took a tablet out of a case she'd left near the door and turned it on. "You're one of *those* Corisis? This is going to be awesome! I can't believe it. Your brother is my newest hero! He's on the cover of every magazine right now. Did you know that he was going to start a revolutionary scholarship fund in China? He's not just talking about it. He's doing it. He's making a difference. What can you tell me about him?"

"I have nothing to say about my brother," Nicole croaked, her throat getting tight with emotion.

Dominic still rang once a day even though she refused to take his calls. She'd had her lawyer contact him regarding Stephan's buyout so he knew that it was no longer necessary for him to be involved in Corisi Ltd. Why couldn't he just leave her alone now?

"Seriously?" Kara's hands dropped to her sides.

"Seriously," Nicole said.

Slipping her tablet back into its protective case, Kara announced, "It's a good thing Mom doesn't want you for her blog."

Nicole raised an eyebrow.

With the brutal honesty of youth, Kara hugged her tablet to her and announced, "You're an awful interview." And she disappeared back into the house.

DINNER WAS A vegetarian delight that all members of the Allen family played a part in creating. When little Kyle handed Stephan a stack of plates, Nicole found hope in the ease in which he performed his delegated responsibility. He

136

and Kyle laughed together as they set the table and Nicole almost burst into hopeful tears.

Is that what he'd look like as a father?

If only we could stay here forever.

Stephan passionately debated the merit of current proposed environmental laws with both the adults and children. Kara and Kyle quoted the voting histories of many politicians like some people quote sport stats.

When the children cross-examined him on if his companies were "green" and what his policies were for waste management, Stephan came alive. Clearly he'd remained true to his core beliefs. Yes, he had walked away from lobbying for the environment, but he'd adhered to stringent polices at all of his companies despite the margin of loss involved.

Kyle asked, "Do you miss making films with my dad?"

Stephan sat back in his chair. "Every day."

Kyle asked, "Then why did you stop?"

"I had some important things that I needed to do."

"More important than global warming?" Kyle asked.

"I thought so at the time." His expression held a hint of regret that Nicole was sure Stephan did not mean to reveal.

"Is that why you don't come visit us? Because it makes you sad to remember?"

Out of the mouths of babes.

Mark said, "Kyle, that's enough."

His wife countered, "Let him ask his questions, Mark. He's not being rude."

Kyle said, "At least I'm asking because I really want to know and not because of some stupid blog."

Kara whined, "Mom, do you hear him?"

Kayla said, "Kyle, you know your sister is sensitive about…"

Stephan cut in, "To answer your question, Kyle... that was exactly why I didn't visit, but I was wrong. I should have come earlier and then you two wouldn't underestimate the value of using strategic litigation to implement environmental laws. It should have been the cornerstone of your debate."

Mark said, "God, it's good to have you around again. You know, we have upcoming projects if you want to be involved in them."

Shaking his head, Stephan said, "I don't have time to camp on location and collect data. There is a lot going on right now."

Organizing some of the used plates into piles, Kayla added, "We don't do most of the legwork anymore, either. We produce the films and use them to help us lobby for change. You always had a good sense of how to frame the message. In fact, some of your old films are still being used to push through change at the state level. Imagine the impact you could make now."

"She's right," Mark interjected. "Your commitment to environmental protection, partnered with your skyrocketing success in the computer business, makes you a voice that would be listened to around the globe."

"I can't really see..." Stephan said.

Mark cut him off and said, "Just think about it."

WHY DID *I agree to this?* Stephan asked himself as he and Nicole entered the guest room that Kayla had prepared for them. It was beautifully decorated in neutral colors, accented by artwork he guessed the children had drawn and Mark'd had professionally framed. A warm and welcoming room, perfect for any other night but tonight.

He and Nicole stood side by side at the foot of the queen-sized bed, neither moving nor speaking at first.

Nicole's voice held a trace of nervous humor. "This didn't seem as awkward when I agreed to it earlier."

Oh, it gets worse. "The door doesn't lock. I checked it when I put the luggage in here," Stephan added blandly.

"I think I can actually hear the kids voices in the other room," Nicole said, looking at the wall just a few feet from the bed.

"Not exactly a mood setter, is it?"

"No," Nicole agreed with a small smile. "Are you disappointed?"

Hell, yes. Stephan almost shared his initial reaction, but then he saw Nicole's expression. She looked vulnerable and hopeful. He reached out and took her hand in his. "Of course I am, but I can survive one night."

"Aren't we here for two?" Nicole asked, surprised.

"Only if we want to be," he growled suggestively. Her gray eyes darkened with desire. He pulled her closer and ran one hand lightly up her spine, tickling her through the thin material of her blouse. If she kept looking at him like that he was going to throw politeness to the wind and drag her off to a hotel tonight.

He pulled her flush against him. She arched her beautiful neck back to look up at him and he couldn't resist. He brought his mouth down on hers. Just a fleeting taste at first but as her lips responded to his, he deepened the kiss.

Nicole's arms slid up his back, clutching him. His tongue seduced her mouth, teasing her to open up more fully to him. She met him, welcomed him, and her soft moan of pleasure almost drove him over the edge.

It would be so easy to forget where they were. He broke off the kiss and the sound of their mutually ragged breathing temporarily blocked out all other sounds. He said, "If we're staying here tonight, this is not a good idea."

"You're right," Nicole agreed, resting her forehead on his chest.

He stroked her upper arms lightly, enjoying the feel of her soft skin. "Going to a hotel now isn't possible either. They wouldn't understand. Well, Mark and Kayla would, but the kids wouldn't."

"We don't want to offend the kids," Nicole agreed breathlessly. She was not making this easy.

She glanced up at him from beneath her long lashes, gray eyes burning with desire and he couldn't resist. He met her eager mouth again. All of the reasons why this was a bad idea flew out of his head. He picked her up, carried her to the bed and rolled with her onto the thick comforter. Her new-found love of simple dresses made access easy, but it wasn't enough. He resented each inch her dress still covered, desperately needing to see all of her, to taste what had been forbidden for so long.

Her devilishly delightful hands unbuttoned his shirt and explored, driving him wild. She slid one just beneath his belt on his lower back. His hands stilled when he realized her intended path. She slid her hand over his hip and he sucked in a breath, unable to think or move, just wait.

"Mom! Kyle commented on my blog again!" Kara's voice echoed down the hallway and was followed by the sound of her stomping to her parents' bedroom.

Nicole laughed softly against his chest and removed her hand. Stephan rolled onto his back and pulled her with him. She was half across him, her hair tumbling down around her face and across his bare chest. She'd never looked more beautiful to him. "You think this is funny?" he growled into her ear.

She smiled down at him and nodded, her eyes brimming with laughter. "I keep expecting Kara to whip the door open."

"We'd end up in her blog." He ran his hand absently through her curtain of black hair.

His body wasn't as quick to downshift as his mind was. It pulsed and punished him. *You're not going to die,* he chided himself. Although, he did vaguely remember this feeling from high school, and had been pretty certain back then that the condition could be fatal. This level of frustration was foreign to his adult life.

As if reading his thoughts, Nicole moved to pull away. Stephan held her to him. "Stay, there. I can control myself."

Cocking her head to one side, Nicole gave him the most adorable, sexy smile and said, "It's not you I'm worried about."

He groaned.

She wants to kill me. She must.

They lay there. Neither moving. Neither speaking.

Quietly wanting.

Nicole asked softly, "Stephan?"

"Yes?"

"I know tonight wasn't what we had planned, but I'm glad we're here. Your friends are very nice people."

Stephan's heart pounded in his chest. His own feelings about the weekend were so tangled up right now that he didn't know what he felt about the trip. He didn't want to be happy that she liked his friends, but he was. Was it too much to hope that his friends would reveal her for a brazen fraud instead of taking him aside to tell him how wonderful she was? Why did she have to be so damn perfect for him? "Yes, they are," he answered absently.

"And their children are incredible – so intelligent."

So, Nicole wants to talk. Ok, let's talk.

"Mark and Kayla believe that knowledge is power, and evidently they've passed that belief on to the next generation." Spending time with the Allen family was bittersweet for Stephan. They were living the life he'd once imagined he'd have.

A healthy marriage. Shared dreams. Amazing kids. They had it all.

And what do I have?

I have this weekend.

Nothing short of Armageddon was going to stop Stephan from whisking Nicole away to the nearest hotel as soon as the boat race concluded tomorrow. He was finally going to have her. Although his blood pounded at the mental image, the feeling of triumph was tainted.

She was his for the weekend. Maybe even for the next few weeks.

Then what?

California was making him crazy. *Then what? Then it ends.* That's what the plan had always been. Imagining any other scenario was unrealistic and dangerous.

Nicole tapped a finger softly on his chest as if she were aware that he'd wandered away in his thoughts. She said, "Kara asked me if I work with a charity."

"Sounds like Kara. What did you say?"

Nicole pushed a lock of hair out of her face. "I said I don't. I never have. How bad of a person am I that I never even thought about it until tonight?"

Why did everything she say only make him hate himself more? "Don't be so hard on yourself, Nicole. You weren't exactly raised by the most generous man."

"But I'm almost thirty, Stephan. How long am I going to blame my father for who I am? When does it become *my* fault?"

"Nicole…"

Nicole shook her head in disagreement to words he had not even yet voiced. "I'm serious. Looking at myself through Kara's eyes was enlightening, to put it nicely. I've spent too much time feeling sorry for myself, thinking only of myself."

The burning sensation in his gut was worse than unfulfilled passion. He didn't want to label it. Some things were better denied even to yourself. "You fought for the top executives at your father's company."

"Because I didn't want to lose them. It was still all about me." He was about to say something, but she rolled off of him and onto her side, tucking one folded arm under her head. "What would you say if I said I want to auction off my father's house with everything in it and donate the proceeds to an abuse shelter?"

He rolled over onto his side, propping his head up on one elbow. "I'd ask you what the hell happened in that house."

Nicole closed her eyes.

Stephan ran a gentle finger across her cheek. "Tell me."

When she opened her eyes, Stephan's entire body tensed with anticipation and fury. Someone had wounded this woman deeply. He'd never seen that expression in her eyes, and realized it was because she'd never let him past her defenses before. This was the Nicole she hid from the world. He was torn between wanting to gather her to him and comfort her, and bolting for the door before it was too late. Instead, he held his breath and waited.

She looked him right in the eye and said, "My father was a violent man. His mood could change as a result of one misspoken word. When we were very little, he only hit my mother. Dominic and I would run to the back of the house when we heard him raise his voice because we knew what was coming. As we got older, Dominic refused to hide, and my father started to take his anger out on him as well." Nicole looked past Stephan and at the wall behind him as if she were revisiting that time in her mind. "I was thirteen when my mother disappeared. The police were at our house every day for a while. They said she had deserted my family, but Dominic imagined something worse. He couldn't let it go. He demanded that my father tell him what had happened to her. Papa tried to intimidate him, but he couldn't scare Dominic anymore so he gave him a choice: stop looking for her or lose everything. Dominic left that night. He said he wouldn't come back until he found our mother."

For the first time, Stephan felt a twinge of admiration for the man he'd hated for so long. Dominic had stood up to a cruel father, a man whom many feared, and had walked away from his own legacy to search for his mother. He didn't want to find anything to like about Dominic. But, the grudging respect was there, nevertheless.

"What happened after Dominic left?" Stephan had to ask. His heart twisted painfully in his chest. *Please tell me it got better. What can I do with so much anger at a man who is unfortunately, untouchably dead?*

"Our family lawyer, Thomas, came to the house and threatened my father. They had been friends since grade school, and Thomas was the only one who ever stood up to Papa. That night they started off yelling at each other and then it got very quiet. I snuck into the hallway to listen.

144

Thomas said there was no place on Earth my father could hide if he laid a hand on me, and that he knew enough about my father's business dealings that he could ruin him if he heard that my father went after Dominic. My father claimed that he hadn't killed my mother, and Thomas said it didn't matter. He said there would be no warning, just retribution if my father stepped out of line."

"But he left you there?" Stephan was having trouble processing the details through his fury.

"Yes," she whispered.

"You must have been so scared," he said, his voice thick with emotion. He pulled her to his chest, breathing harshly into her hair. She neither refused his embrace nor returned it, too lost in her memories to do either.

"I was at first, but my father never even raised his voice at me after that. Something inside him died that year. There were no more bad times, but there were no good times either. I even tried to get him angry at me once. I thought, at least if he hit me he would have to look at me while he did it. But he just walked away like he couldn't see me. I just wanted him to see me."

Stephan tucked her head beneath his chin, feeling her silent tears through the light material of his shirt. "I wish ..." He groaned and buried his face in her hair. If he had known, he would have been kinder to her when she'd come to his office to ask for help. He wouldn't have been so quick to believe the worst of her seven years ago. "I didn't know, Nicole. If I had known…"

Nicole leaned back and placed a comforting hand on his jaw. Her cheeks were wet with memories and her eyes stormed with emotion. "It wouldn't have done any good. I wouldn't have left my father. I hated him so much, but I loved him, too. When word came that my mother had died,

Dominic became obsessed with tearing down everything our father had built. His constant attack on our father made me protective of Papa. Crazy, huh? I hated my father, but I thought he needed me. Dominic should have been my hero for standing up to him, but I did whatever I could to protect my father. Why would I do that?"

"Because he was your father."

Nicole shook her head sadly. "I'm not sorry that he's dead so painting me as a loving daughter is a stretch. I'm just glad it's over. Maybe now I can move on. I don't want to be angry or afraid anymore. I want to surround myself with genuine, loving people. I can't change my childhood, but I can choose who is part of my life today." She caressed his jaw absently. "People like you and your family. Good people."

Her words cut him to the core. *Not like me.* Once upon a time, he might have been the man she was looking for, but not any longer.

He eased his arms from around her and said, "It's late, Nicole. Go to sleep."

A worried frown creased her forehead. "Did I say something wrong?"

Stephan turned off the lamp beside the bed. "No, I'm just tired." He flipped onto his side, facing away from her.

"Ok," she said slowly, hurt evident in her voice. She rolled over and on to her side of the bed.

Stephan waited until her breathing deepened and he was sure she was asleep. Then he eased off the bed and sat in a chair in the corner of the room. As he watched her sleep, the weight of his guilt settled over him. He had no right to sleep with her when she came to him honestly and openly, not when he knew that there was no way their reunion could withstand what he had set into motion.

She had endured and survived.

Coming to California with her had been a mistake. Staying and leading Nicole on for the rest of the weekend would be an even bigger one. Tomorrow morning, he'd say that he'd received an emergency call from New York—a problem at work that only he could solve. Then, as soon as they returned, Stephan would initiate the paperwork to transfer Corisi Ltd back to Nicole, and announce that they'd broken off their engagement. The sooner he got her out of his life, the better it would be for both of them.

A perfect plan with only one flaw. Stephan layed back against the chair and closed his eyes in resignation.

I love her.

CHAPTER *Sixteen*

SUNDAY MORNING, NICOLE sat at the small table in Stephan's kitchen – alone. Yesterday, he had rushed both of them back to NY so he could deal with some upper-management emergency. He'd sent her back to his penthouse in a limo and had headed off to his office. She'd waited up for him past midnight, but he hadn't returned. So, here she sat, all alone, with the breakfast for two the cook had prepared.

Her driver called from downstairs, but instead of going down, she asked him to come up. He took a long look at her pajamas before saying, "So, not going out today?"

"No."

"Boycotting the shower, too?"

"Maybe. Want a coffee?" she gestured to the cup that was going to waste.

"That bad, huh?" Jeff asked, joining her at the table.

Nicole pulled both feet up onto the chair with her and hugged her legs. "I messed up in California."

Jeff pushed Stephan's scrambled eggs around the plate a few times before shrugging and having a few forkfuls. "What's your definition of messed up?"

"Everything was going smoothly. His friends were great. He and I were connecting. We kissed. It was hot. I mean the best kiss I've ever had. I've had sex before, but this…"

Jeff cut in, "Just get to the part where you messed up."

"I told him about my family."

"And?"

"And he barely talked to me on the flight back. He didn't come home last night. I don't want to call him because he said our early return was work-related."

"But?"

"But I don't believe him. He looked miserable yesterday. It wasn't like he didn't care when I told him the story, but afterwards he wouldn't look at me. I don't know what that means."

Jeff took a sip of the cold coffee then put it down. "It's either a good sign or really bad."

Nicole almost smiled. "Wow, you are helpful."

Jeff pushed out of his seat and stood. "I'm not psychic if that's what you were hoping for. But if you want to know what he's thinking there is one way you could find out."

Nicole dropped her feet to the floor and stood. *I'm getting desperate enough to try anything.* "Yes?"

Jeff said, "*Ask him.* I'll be downstairs if you need me." He closed the door quietly behind him.

An hour later, dressed in yoga pants, a t-shirt and sneakers, Nicole headed out the main door of the apartment building. There was a small coffee shop about a block away. The sun was shining. *Maybe a walk will clear my head.*

Jeff was right. Instead of dancing around the topic, afraid to offend or anger anyone, maybe she should just ask him.

Love is possible if you are willing to fight for it. Wasn't that what Maddy always said?

So, why do I keep accepting everything without an argument? I could have asked Stephan these questions on the flight home. I could have demanded that he tell me why we were really coming back to New York. If I wasn't still afraid.

What am I afraid of?

Losing him? He's already headed out the door.

Angering him? Stephan is not my father. He would never hurt me.

She had only gone a few yards when a woman who looked vaguely familiar approached her. Lost in her thoughts, she barely noticed her at first.

"Nicole?"

"I'm sorry, do I know you?"

"My name is Abby Dartley. We've met before. Once, at the reading of your father's will."

Nicole held her breath then let it out slowly. "Oh, yes, my brother's new fiancé. Congratulations, I guess."

The woman was dressed in simple, yet exclusive slacks and a conservative blouse. Two men watched from beside a limo across the street, one to drive and one to guard. Abby didn't seem bothered by their presence. It sure hadn't taken her long to get used to her new level of wealth.

"Can we go somewhere to talk?" the woman asked.

Nicole looked down at her watch. *Why the hell not? It's not like my week could get worse.* "I was going to get a quick coffee. You can walk with me if you want."

Abby stepped closer and fell into stride with her. "Dominic has been trying to call you."

"I know."

Once inside the coffee shop, they suspended conversation until they had their order and were seated at a corner table away from prying ears. Abby seemed in no rush to break the awkward silence between them. Nicole said, "Well, spit out whatever you came to say. What does Dominic want?"

Abby didn't ruffle as easily as Nicole thought she would. "Your brother is really worried about you."

Nicole looked down at her coffee. "Tell him he doesn't have to be."

"He loves you, Nicole. He might not be good at showing it, but..."

Eyes snapping up to meet Abby's, Nicole said, "You've known him...what? a month? I've known him my whole life. He only cares about one thing – Dominic."

"That's not true. He let you down. He knows that, but he would give anything for a chance to make it up to you."

"Is that what he told you? That he *let me down*? Does he think an apology will cover what he did? First, he deserted me like our mother had, and then, just when I thought I might have found a family who cared about me, he ripped them away from me, too. I'm sure he didn't tell you that last part," Nicole spat out the words.

Abby didn't flinch. Her voice remained smooth with a soothing undertone that Nicole fought against. "He did tell me. Neither is something that he is very proud of doing. He was only 17 when your mother left, barely a man. You can't hate him for the decisions he made fifteen years ago."

"And what about the Andrade family? Did he have to take their company? Their island? Did he have to build that chrome monstrosity on it, and rub his lack of respect for their heritage in their faces? Did he do that out of his *love* for me?"

"No," Abby said sadly. "I bet he doesn't even know why he did that. He acted out of jealousy, and he was wrong. He's stubborn and he's proud, but he would never deliberately hurt you. Give him a chance to apologize."

"He's had 15 years to do that. It's a little late now. I want to move on." Nicole stood.

Abby also stood and looked like she wanted to wrap her arms around Nicole. "It's ok to feel like that, Nicole. But Dominic is there for you if you need him. We both are. One phone call, and you'll see that he would do anything for you."

Nicole dropped her still full coffee into the trash. Her stomach was nervous and sour. "Sweet as you are to come here and plead his case, I have no desire to see him ever again. You can tell him that I absolve him from whatever guilt he is carrying from our childhood. I don't hate him anymore, but I don't need him either."

"I understand, but we're staying here in New York. We're not going anywhere." She passed Nicole a paper with her phone number on it. "Keep this in case you change your mind."

Nicole took it and said, "Why do you care? What do you get out of this?"

Abby's eyes welled with tears. "Hopefully, another sister." And she walked away.

CHAPTER *Seventeen*

SUNDAY NIGHT, NICOLE waited up for Stephan. They needed to talk. She'd come to some decisions that would affect both of them.

After leaving the coffee shop, Nicole had taken a long walk in Central Park. The fresh air and sunshine had gone mostly unnoticed as she'd woven her way through the large number of people who'd also decided to enjoy the warm, summer day.

Before heading back, she'd stopped at Belvedere Castle to look out over Turtle Pond. She and Dominic had gone there many times as young children. It was their favorite destination with their mother when some function had necessitated Papa bringing them to the city. The Corisis didn't have nannies either, but for more nefarious reasons. Cleaning services could be scheduled and canceled with no need to interact with the family. Nannies would have seen too much.

Playing on the rocks behind the castle, Nicole used to pretend she was a princess trapped in a dungeon by an evil

153

dragon. In their shared fantasy, Dominic had always slain the dragon and set her free.

Is that what I hold against him? That in the end, he wasn't a hero—just a man?

And the only family I truly have left.

George and the others were people that she cared about, and that she was lucky enough to have return that affection, but they weren't family.

The Andrades were everything she'd ever dreamt of in a family, but they weren't hers. Not yet. Maybe not ever.

No matter what had happened between them, Dominic was her brother.

Abby said he loved her and Nicole was starting to believe he might.

He had called her every day since she'd seen him at the reading of the will, and although she hadn't once taken his phone call, he hadn't given up. What if Abby was right and he regretted everything, just like she did? Could they reach across the years of hurt and mend their family? Or was it too late?

Nicole jumped at the click of the door opening. Stephan was home.

He wasn't going to like what she had to tell him, but maybe that was what they needed—simple honesty. No more trying to trick him into doing something she wanted. No more hiding how she felt. If they couldn't talk – really talk – then they had nothing worth fighting for.

She met him in the hallway while he was still taking off his jacket and loosening his tie. He looked like he hadn't slept since she last saw him. "You didn't come home last night," she said, attempting to keep her tone neutral.

"Yeah," he ran a hand through his already tousled, blond hair. "Sorry about that. I had to get some things done."

"Really?" she asked, following him into the living room. "I don't believe you."

He kept his back to her. "Don't push it, Nicole."

She stepped in front of him and looked him directly in the eye. "I am going to *push it*. I have a right to know what happened. Before California, I thought we were at least friends. Then at the Allen's house we connected. I didn't imagine that. So, what changed? Why won't you look at me?"

"Why can't you just drop it?" his voice rose with each word.

Nicole's body tensed, but the fear did not come. This was not her father. She had nothing to fear here. Still, part of her journey was realizing that she played a role in how she was treated. "Do not raise your voice at me, Stephan. I won't be yelled at."

His face twisted with an emotion she couldn't determine. "I would never hit you, Nicole."

"I know," Nicole said softly and she believed him. His family was loud, but they weren't cruel. She stepped closer to him. "I trust you, Stephan."

He stepped back and away from her. "Don't. I'm not the man you think I am, Nicole. I wish I were. I wanted to have sex with you, that's it. That's all there could ever be between us."

His hands were clenched at his sides and there was so much emotion in his eyes that Nicole didn't believe him. If he was telling her the truth, if she meant nothing to him, why did he look tormented by his own declarations?

He said, "I realized in California, that you were right when you said that this should be a purely business arrangement, Nicole, and nothing more. Sex is just going to confuse a situation that will soon be over anyway."

Nicole took a step toward him. "It doesn't have to be that way, Stephan."

His blue eyes raged with something he wouldn't or couldn't tell her. "Yes, it does."

Why won't you look at me? There wasn't much further they could go with that conversation that evening, so she changed topics. "I called my brother."

Stephan head whipped up. "Why?"

I have to do this, even if it means losing you again. Nicole clasped her cold hands in front of herself. "I'm meeting him tomorrow at my father's house. I can't spend the rest of my life hating him for what my father did to our family."

Stephan said nothing. He was shaking his head ever so slightly.

Nicole continued. "This doesn't change anything. I won't tell him that we're not really engaged and you'll still get the patent."

"I don't want the patent," he said harshly and turned away from her again.

"But that's why you did all this, wasn't it? Partly because I had helped Maddy, and also because you knew you would profit from the conversion software?" She laid a hand on his back, wordlessly begging him to turn around. His muscles jumped beneath her touch.

"Go see your brother, Nicole," he said and stepped away from her. Before she had time to ask him another question, he'd retreated to his room and closed the door.

CHAPTER *Eighteen*

MONDAY MORNING, NICOLE ate breakfast alone again before calling Jeff to take her to her father's old house. She'd considered various locations where she and her brother could meet. Finally, she'd decided that they should return to where it had all begun.

Nicole had just opened the front door that led to a large main foyer of her father's house when Dominic's limo pulled into the driveway and parked behind hers. She watched him exit it then turn to offer an arm to Abby. He spoke to her as if preparing Abby for what was to come, and then leaned down and kissed her gently before taking her hand and walking with her toward the house.

He loves her. He really loves her.

Nicole stepped into the house and waited for them in the foyer. The three of them endured a painfully long silence until Nicole said, "Thank you for coming."

"Did you think I wouldn't?" Dominic asked roughly.

Abby slid beneath his arm and hugged him. She was a welcome buffer. Nicole and Dominic had never been good at making small talk.

Nicole offered a truce. "I wouldn't have blamed you if you hadn't."

Abby looked around at the boxes that were in every adjoining room. "Are you moving?"

"Yes. I've decided to auction off the house and its contents. So, if there is anything you want, Dominic, take it now. The auction house is sending someone to do the evaluation and the real cataloguing, but they asked that we make sure that when we said everything must go that we meant *everything*."

Dominic scowled. "There is nothing here I want."

Nicole said, "I feel the same way." She hesitated, then added, "I'm giving the proceeds to a local abuse shelter."

Abby said, "That is a beautiful thing to do."

"It seemed...appropriate. I've decided that it's time to let go of the past."

Dominic— strong, ruthless Dominic, flushed and his eyes shone with emotion. He stepped toward Nicole then seemed to rethink the move and stopped. "I am so sorry, Nicole. So very sorry that I wasn't the brother you needed."

Nicole clasped her hands together, fighting to retain her composure. "He damaged us both, Dominic."

Never one to hedge, Dominic said, "I want to make it up to you. I need to make it up to you."

With reflection came understanding. "I don't think you can, Dominic, and maybe our healing starts when I accept that. The past is done. We should bury it along with Papa."

"So where will that leave us?" he asked, sounding almost humble.

"I don't know. I never thought we'd get this far."

There was no hugging. It was too early to do more than look across the chasm at each other and acknowledge that neither and both of them had been at fault.

"I should have come back for you, Nicole," the words were wrenched from him.

"And I should have left when I was old enough. We can't change the mistakes we've already made." Loving someone involved forgiving them for not being perfect, but Nicole was learning that it also involved forgiving yourself.

Dominic took another step toward Nicole, determination hardening his features. "No, but we can make damn sure we don't repeat them. Nicole, you can't marry Stephan."

Wham.

The door that had just begun to open between them slammed shut. Nicole spun away. "Don't talk about Stephan."

Dominic strode to stand in front of her. "I know you don't want to hear it, but whatever he told you...however he convinced you to get engaged to him...he's using you. I don't know what he thinks he will gain by doing this, but he's lying to you."

Abby broke in, "Dominic, we don't know that for sure."

Dominic snarled, "You might not, but I do. He's using her to get to me."

A spark of anger ignited into a slow burning fury. Nicole advanced until she was toe to toe with her brother. Her voice shook with emotion. "So, my entire relationship with him is about *you*, Dominic? It can't be about me, right? He can't *love me*? It all has to be about the great Dominic Corisi."

"That's not what I'm saying, Nicole. I just don't want to see him hurt you."

159

"Hurt me? Stephan *saved* me. You know what, our engagement isn't even real. He did it as a favor to me. Imagine. He cared enough about me to not only play along, but also to put his own money into the deal, risking his reputation, for *me.* And what did he ask for in return? Nothing. Because he's not like you, Dominic. He doesn't play by your rules. He's a good man. A decent man." Angry tears began to spill down her cheeks.

"I don't believe that Stephan wanted nothing from you." Dominic's face went red with anger.

"That's because you judge him by your standards. But he's not you. He stands by his family and his friends. And even after everything you did to him—to us—he helped me when I asked him to. So don't tell me what you *think* you know about him."

Dominic's phone rang. He answered it and said roughly,"No, that's not a good idea. She can't handle it today. Stay in the limo."

"Can't handle what?"

"It's nothing. Nothing we need to get into today."

"More lies? How are we going to put the past behind us if we still can't be honest with each other?"

Abby jumped in, physically standing between Nicole and the door. "I have to agree with Dominic on this one, Nicole. Not today."

A red haze blurred Nicole's vision as a sickening possibility grabbed hold of her. It couldn't be. "Just who the hell is in that limo? *Who, Dominic?"*

Nicole pushed past Abby and Dominic and rushed down the stone stairs to the vehicles. She marched over to Dominic's limo. *The lies end today.* She opened the door and slammed it just as quickly.

160

"Get me out of here, now, Jeff," Nicole said from within the safety of her own limo.

He floored the gas and hit the control for the gate ahead to open. Although he was driving forward, his attention remained on the scene unfolding in the driveway behind them. "Are you sure, because there is a whole crowd of people running after us...even some older woman."

Nicole clutched her stomach with both hands. "I'm sure. That woman is my long deceased mother. Unless you want to see me completely lose my mind, I'd beat them to the gate."

He sped off. "Are you sure that was your mother and not a cousin or a..."

"Twin? No, that was my mother. There are some things you just know. Oh my god, my mother is still alive. I should be happy, right? I mean, she's not dead. Why isn't she dead? Dominic said all of his investigators reported she'd died in Italy over ten years ago. Why would he lie?"

Jeff interjected in his infuriatingly reasonable tone, "These sound like questions we could get the answers to if we turned around and asked them."

Nicole burst into angry laughing, crying tears. "My mother is not dead." *My mother is not dead.* She repeated the words in her head as they birthed even more unwelcome realizations. "She just didn't want me either. I liked her better when she was dead."

They cleared the gate and Jeff took several random turns in case anyone was following. No one did. "Where do you want me to drive to?"

There was really only one place left to go. "Take me to Stephan's office building."

Jeff glanced back at her in his rearview mirror. "I'm not sure you should go like this."

The cold anger bubbling in Nicole's stomach left no room for debate. She had to know. "Dominic said Stephan had another reason to help me—a reason that had nothing to do with me and everything to do with getting back at Dominic."

Jeff asked, "And you think he's going to tell you?"

Nicole folded her arms across her chest. "Oh, he'll tell me. I'm going to wring the truth out of that bastard."

CHAPTER *Nineteen*

"NICOLE MUST BE really good in bed, because you, my friend, have become delusional."

"Leave Nicole out of this." Stephan hissed. "Can you remove the virus? I don't care how much it costs, is the process reversible?"

"I don't think you get what I'm telling you. I don't want to reverse it. I bugged his system to become famous within the world of hackers, within the world of *anonymous* hackers. Not to become infamous for being stupid enough to try to get back into that program to undo it. This isn't a game. There isn't an off switch."

"Things have changed. I can't go through with this anymore."

"Nothing has changed for me. When Dominic uploads his software next month, it's going to be so full of server issues he'll be the laughing stock of the software community, and I will be set for life."

"I can't let you do it."

"It's too late, Stephan. It's done and I'm not taking the fall because your dick found your conscience for you. Don't call me again. If I get caught, you're the one who will pay the price. I'm the little guy in this drama. Who do they want splashed across the news for putting in prison? Some computer geek no one knows...or you, Stephan? Think about it. If caught, I'll probably end up working for some government agency helping them look for software vulnerabilities while you rot in jail. Don't call me again."

The phone line went dead.

Stephan caught his reflection in the mirror across the room and hated what he saw. How had he gotten to this place? When had saving the environment and then his family become this?

He'd become the man he had set out to destroy.

If only Nicole had been as cunning and as contemptible as he'd once thought her to be, he could have walked away from her at the end of this. *But, no.* She had to be the kind of woman a man feels he must protect – even from himself.

She didn't really hate her brother and that made what he had done so much worse.

He was going to have to tell her.

Somehow.

NICOLE WAS FINISHED with the lies. Finished with the games. Either Stephan had feelings for her, or he didn't.

She stormed into his office.

"I love you," she said defiantly. "I have loved you since you pestered me to go out on a date with you seven years ago. I loved you even when I thought you hated me. And these three weeks together have been some of the best times of my life. But I need to know if you are lying to me,

Stephan. Is any of it real? Do you love me or is this some sick game of revenge with my brother? I need to know the truth. I deserve the truth. Dominic thinks this is all about him. Tell me he's wrong."

She stood before his desk, finally releasing a breath, and waited.

Nicole felt like she'd been kicked in the chest when he didn't answer. He just sat there looking as guilty as hell. "You...bastard. When were you going to tell me?"

He lifted an awkward shoulder, "It didn't matter in the beginning why I said yes, did it? You were using me as much as I was using you."

"And what exactly did being engaged to me get you?" He almost said something, but she interrupted him. "No, I don't want to know. I'm done with all of it. You, my brother, all the lies. I can't handle all the lies."

"Nicole, I..."

"What? Are you going to tell me that you love me, too? " She laughed without humor. "Why the hell not? Say it. Even if it's a lie it doesn't matter...I don't seem to know anyone who tells the truth."

She spun on her heel to leave.

He beat her to the door. "Where are you going?" he demanded.

"I don't know, but don't pretend to care." When he reached for her, she evaded his touch and snarled, "Don't touch me. Don't ever touch me again."

Dry-eyed, Nicole walked out of his office and took the elevator down to where Jeff and the limo were waiting. She was done crying.

"Where to?" Jeff asked.

"Aren't you going to ask how it went?" she asked tiredly.

Pulling out into traffic, Jeff shook his head. "Not really. Nope."

Nicole smacked the seat next to her. "Dominic was right. It was all about some stupid rivalry between the two of them. Stephan never loved me. I doubt he even cares about me. It's all a game to them. That's probably why Dominic kept calling me. He wanted to win and this time I was the prize." Getting angrier the more she thought about it, she turned on Jeff. "*You* think you know everything. Am I right? Was this whole thing nothing more than a contest between two over-inflated egos? Well? Nothing to say this time, Jeff? Where is your pithy advice?"

Jeff's shoulders slumped a bit. "I'm sorry it turned out this way for you, Nicole. That's it. I'm just sorry you have to go through this."

Nicole relaxed into her seat. None of this was his fault. "Me, too, Jeff. Me, too."

"WHERE IS MY father?" Stephan asked the uncle who greeted him an instant after a member of their house staff had announced him.

Alessandro's easy smile was replaced by a quick look of concern, but he didn't voice his questions. "Victor is reading in my study."

Stephan started walking away, but his uncle's voice stopped his progress. "Stephan, I'm out here if you need me."

If only I deserved his support.

Without turning, Stephan said, "I know. Thank you."

Reclining in his favorite leather chair, one that had remained in the US for him to visit, Victor closed the newspaper at the sound of Stephan's approach. His father

166

was as comfortable here in Alessandro's home as he was in his villa in Italy, and Victor took pride in the knowledge that his brother felt equally at home in either.

Stephan stopped and stood humbly before his father's chair, unable to meet his father's eyes, in a way he hadn't since childhood—not since he'd broken a guest's car window and gone to confess.

But this was worse.

Much worse.

"Dad, I need to talk to you."

He didn't have to tell his father how serious it was. Victor's asked urgently, "What is it? Nicole? Did you two have a fight?"

Stephan met his father's eyes with a sad shake of his head. "I wish it were that simple, Dad. I am going to tell you something that will change what you think of me."

"Are you sure it needs to be said?" Victor laid the newspaper on the floor beside his chair.

"I have to tell someone."

Victor stood and laid a supportive hand on Stephan's shoulder. "It's never as bad as we think it is."

Oh, sometimes it is.

"I helped a hacker upload a virus to Dominic Corisi's Chinese server. I used my connections to get his access codes."

Victor sat down in his chair with a heavy thud, his face suddenly pinched and white.

Yeah, that's what I thought. There was no defense for what he'd done, only an explanation. "I was angry about losing the deal and I thought he deserved it. As soon as Dominic puts his software online, he'll lose everything."

"Stephan." He'd never heard such disappointment in his father's voice, and it tore at him. "How could you do this?"

I've asked myself that same question a thousand times.

Stephan strode over to look out the study window, unable to see anything except his father's pained expression which would forever haunt him. "I don't know, Dad. I got so wrapped up in winning that I agreed to something that I knew was wrong."

"Does Nicole know?"

It didn't even occur to Stephan to lie. "She knows I used her to get back at her brother, but she doesn't know more than that. No one does. There probably isn't a way to trace this back to me."

"So why are you telling me this, Stephan?" He'd expected his father to be angry. He was prepared for that. He didn't know how to handle the regret he heard in his father's voice, the unwavering love still evident in his tone.

"Because I won. I finally beat Dominic."

"But?"

His father knew him too well.

"But I can't live with the knowledge that I hurt Nicole by doing this. She has endured so many betrayals. She stormed into my office today and announced that she loved me. She wanted to know if I had betrayed her, too. I wanted so badly to say that I hadn't, but I had. I tried to undo what I've done, but it's too late. I'm no better than her family was to her. She came to me for help and I used her." Stephan turned and looked his father in the eye.

The two remained motionless and silent until Stephan couldn't bear it anymore. He said, "Say something, Dad. Say anything."

The older man rubbed one of his knees absently as if trying to ease an old pain. "I wish I knew what to say. I wish none of this were my fault."

Stephan's head shot back in response to the distasteful idea. "Your fault? None of this is your fault. You're the kind of man I wish I were."

His proud father shook his head sadly. "No, Stephan. We all have our flaws. Mine are becoming clearer to me with age."

"What are you saying, Dad?"

Victor stood and faced his son. "You were a good son, Stephan. You did everything I asked when you were young. I thought you would take over the company when you were old enough, but after college, I saw you drifting away to California. Drifting away from me, the family, the business. All you cared about was making films with your friends. I saw no future in that."

"It's ok, Dad. That was a long time ago. It doesn't matter anymore."

His father's face tightened with anger. "No, it does matter. I should have let you be the man you wanted to be. You were happy in that life. Maybe you and Nicole would have married and had children by now if I had not interfered."

"I don't understand."

His father continued, "The economy was taking a nose dive; I was tired. I wanted to retire and you were indifferent to the company...so, I approached Dominic. Andrade Solutions was already in the red. It wasn't worth what I had hoped. Half of our family worked for me. Not like now with Alessandro running his own business. I had convinced them all to follow me here to the US and make this new life for ourselves. I had to give everyone enough money to start fresh. I owed them that. So, I included Isola Santos in the deal. Dominic didn't swindle me out of it. I sold it to him and split the money between the families."

Stephan rocked back with shock. "Why, Dad? Why would you go to Dominic of all people?"

"He could easily afford to buy out my company, and I was angry with you. You were living your life carelessly. You'd found a woman the family adored, and you were propositioning her like some common tramp. I knew that involving her brother would end it between the two of you." He looked away. "I wanted you to grow up."

"All this time, I blamed Dominic…"

His father looked older suddenly. "I know. In the beginning, I thought having an adversary would be good for you. And for a while, it was. You moved home, and before I knew it you'd started your own computer company. I had no idea how strongly you and Dominic would clash, and by the time I realized that you had genuinely cared for Nicole, it was too late."

Stephan swayed beneath the news. This changed everything. He'd spent seven years obsessing over an event that had never happened. Dominic hadn't stolen anything.

And more importantly – Nicole was innocent.

What have I done?

"I am sorry, son. This is my fault."

"No," Stephan said. He was a better man because of his time with Nicole. He could hear her voice in his head. *You're thirty-one years old, Stephan, time to take responsibility for your own mistakes.*

Stephan said, "You may have set this in motion, Dad, but I could have let Nicole explain back then instead driving her off with my accusations. I could have stopped this obsession at any time over the last seven years. I did this. I took it too far."

Victor asked softly, "You do love Nicole, don't you?"

Truth was the antiseptic this entire situation required – even if it stung. "Yes, but our engagement was just a cover, Dad."

"I know. Alessandro finally told me."

"How did he know?"

Maddy!

"If you all knew it wasn't true—why did everyone play along?" It didn't make any sense.

Victor answered with a one-shoulder shrug. "Nicole is the kind of woman we'd all like to see you with. She's got a heart the size of Italy and anyone who has been around the two of you for even a second can see that you're crazy about each other."

Stephan slumped a bit in defeat. "She's gone, Dad. I screwed up and lost her."

Resting a supportive hand on his son's shoulder again, Victor said, "That doesn't sound like the son I know. You've never given up on anything you cared about."

Stephan met his father's eyes. "This isn't something I can simply apologize for."

His father nodded. "You're right. How much are you willing to risk to get her back?"

Anything. Everything.

"I could go to jail for this, Dad."

His father squeezed his shoulder. "That's true and that's why I can't tell you what to do here. I won't betray your secret, no matter what you decide."

Stephan bit back a question. The answer didn't really matter anyway.

Victor caught his son's expression and asked, "What do you want to know, Stephan?"

The question jumped out of him. "Why aren't you yelling at me that I've ruined everything? We'll never get Isola Santos back now."

Shaking his head, Victor said, "Stephan, you think our legacy is really a rock in the ocean? How we treat our wives, our children…even our enemies – *that* is our legacy. You did something you never should have done, but you still have time to fix it. I don't want to see you go to jail, Stephan, but I fear for who you will become if you don't make this right."

Stephan straightened and announced, "I have to stop the virus from taking down Dominic's server."

His father nodded slowly.

Stephan hugged his father tightly. He had never had more respect for his father than he did at this moment. Any good Stephan had left in him was because of the strength and integrity of the man who had raised him. If he survived this folly, Stephan was going to spend the rest of his life trying to live up to his example.

"Where are you going?" his father asked when Stephan stepped away from him.

Stephan paused at the door, not turning back from his course. "I'm going to see Dominic. He's the only one who can stop this now."

As he walked out the door, he heard his father say, "Now *that* is my son."

CHAPTER *Twenty*

NICOLE SAT IN her father's old leather chair behind his huge mahogany desk.

How did I get here? There must have been a time when I was happy.

She remembered back to before her mother had left, a time between her father's fits of anger, when she'd visited him here with her mother. She'd been so proud of her strong father. He'd commanded those around him like a king with his army, and this chair had been his throne, one that he'd let her climb up into and use to reach the intercom to order a glass of milk from the secretary. No, she hadn't always been miserable.

That revelation didn't provide the answers she desperately needed.

Why would her mother come back now and where had she been all this time?

Had Dominic meant anything he'd said about wanting to be part of her life again?

How could I have been so wrong about Stephan?

Nicole smoothed her hands over the surface of her father's desk and another question came to her. *Is this really where I want to be?*

She'd sat with the board of directors for two weeks of meetings, running her father's company, waiting for a feeling of euphoria to hit, but it never had. Even as she negotiated new contracts and strategized on how to get the red bottom line to green, there was no pleasure in it for her.

I don't really care about computers or software design. How did I not know this about myself?

Nicole looked at her father's office, at her father's company, with a fresh perspective. It was all her father's dream, not hers.

Until now, I was so busy trying to be the person I thought I should be that I never asked myself who I want to be.

In the beginning, learning about computers had been all about winning her father's love, and saving the company had been more out of the fear of losing the few people she was close to rather a desire to work in the corporate world.

She picked up the phone and called someone she knew she could trust. Someone who had always stood by her. "George, how do you feel about choosing a new CEO? No, I'm not taking a vacation, I'm switching careers." He wasn't surprised and only had one question. "What am I going to do?" She thought about her abuse shelter auction and said, "I don't know, but it's going to be in the non-profit sector."

DOMINIC WAS NOT alone in his office. The ever-present Jake was leaning on a book case; close enough to hear the conversation, but far enough away to be an observer.

Stephan walked in with the determination of a man who wasn't leaving before he'd set things right.

Surprisingly, Dominic had included his fiancé in this meeting. She stood at his side, holding his hand, which was likely the only reason why it wasn't already wrapped around Stephan's throat.

"Stephan," Dominic said in a less than warm greeting. "I'd ask you to sit, but I really don't want this to take any longer than necessary. You said you had information for me. Something that couldn't be said over the phone."

Stephan braced himself mentally and said, "There is no way to make this sound good so I'm just going to say it. Your Chinese server has been hacked and I'm responsible. Don't put it online next month until you've completely debugged it and run extensive tests here."

Dominic's face went bright red, then cold white. He took a threatening step toward Stephan, who didn't back away. "I'm going to kill you."

Abby got between them, one hand up on either chest. "Dominic, hitting him is not going to solve anything"

"I'm not just going to hit him..."

Stephan said, "Let him go, I deserve it."

Dominic wholeheartedly agreed. "Yes, you do."

Jake pushed away from the wall and joined the trio. "Why did you come here, Stephan? Why tell us?"

Dominic snarled, "Did you slip up? Someone found out and you think that things will go easier for you if you come clean first?"

Stephan stood perfectly still, hands casually buried in his pants pockets. "No, I did it perfectly. There's no way to trace it back to me, no one who would benefit from exposing my involvement."

Jake pressed for more. "Then why confess? Is this blackmail? You've got the code to fix it?"

"No, I wish I did. In fact, I'm not even sure it can be fixed."

"You just wanted to die young?" Dominic ground the words out.

Abby lowered her hands and said, "Is this about Nicole?"

Dominic said, "If it is, you're a fool. You're going to spend so much time in prison she'll be in a nursing home by the time you get out."

Stephan's shoulders slumped somewhat. It was no more than he deserved. "I completely understand if you call the police, Dominic. I would have done it if our situations were reversed."

Abby asked urgently, "Stephan, where is she?"

All or nothing. "I haven't seen her since yesterday. She said she loved me and she asked me if I had an ulterior motive for helping her. I wanted to say no, but I had used the fake engagement with Nicole to distract Dominic so he wouldn't push for more software testing until it was too late. And it worked. I just didn't know..."

Abby finished the sentence for him. "That you would fall in love with her."

Stephan said, "Exactly. Listen, I know she never wants to see me again..."

Dominic growled, "Good. Because you've got about as much chance of seeing her as you do of staying solvent once this news gets out."

Jake interceded again, a voice of reason amid the threats. "Dom, hang on. Think this through. We probably don't want anyone to know about the virus. Not unless you want China to get nervous and pull out of the deal. If we keep this quiet, we can fix it in-house."

Dominic took another threatening step toward Stephan. "Does anyone else know?"

Stephan didn't back down. He didn't hate Dominic anymore, but he wasn't going to cower before him either. "No."

Dominic's fists clenched. "Don't think this lets you off the hook. You're going down for this...if not through the legal system then..."

Abby got between the two of them again and threw up her hands in exasperation. "Enough! Enough already. What is with you two? You're like two little kids fighting over a toy in the sandbox. Now that we know about the virus, we'll fix it, but the bigger question is *where is Nicole?* Yesterday she found out that her dead mother is alive, and that the man she loves was using her. That's not good. We've got to find her."

Stephan leaned in, unconsciously threatening Dominic. "Her mother is alive? And you knew?"

Dominic faltered before recovering and glared back at him. "She's my mother, too. I've only known for a few weeks. We were trying to find a good way to tell Nicole about her."

That's a laugh. "You? Find a good way? If you hurt her..." Stephan's hands clenched at his sides.

Dominic mirrored Stephan's aggressive stance. "You are the *last* person who should talk about hurting Nicole."

The only real question was who would swing first.

Abby looked back and forth between them, and brought out what must have been her teacher tone. "Seriously, you two need to stop it right now. This is not about either of you. It's about Nicole. Where would she go?"

Dominic deflated somewhat and sounded apologetic when he met his fiancé's indignant look. His tone was comically gentle. "I'll call Thomas. Maybe he heard from her."

Abby turned to Stephan. "I bet you know where she'd go."

Stephan released the breath he'd been unconsciously holding and said, "Not exactly, but I know who would."

OUTSIDE OF DOMINIC'S office building, Stephan said, "Thanks for coming, Jeff."

Jeff stood near the door of the limo and said, "I wasn't sure I'd heard you right when you gave me the address."

"Do you know where Nicole is, Jeff?"

"I might."

"Might?"

"It depends on what exactly this is..." He pointed to Dominic, Abby and Jake standing behind him.

"We want to make sure she's ok," Stephan said. *I need to know she's ok.*

"I'm not sure any of you are qualified to make that determination."

"Unlike you? Just who the hell do you think you are?" Stephan roared.

Jeff shrugged. "Just the limo driver who knows where she is." He stood his ground, unwavering with the confidence of youth.

Stephan threw both hands in the air. "I love her and I've made some serious mistakes that hurt her, but she shouldn't be alone right now." As awful as it was for him to admit it, Stephan said, "Even if she doesn't need me, she needs her family. You know that."

Jeff nodded, apparently satisfied by something he saw. "But don't rush in there all together. Yesterday sent her running, but she's working it out. If you really do love her, she's hurting and could use the support. But if this is just more of the competition between you and Dominic, do her a favor and stay the hell away from her."

Stephan wanted more than anything to go to Nicole, to go and beg her to forgive him. But odd as it was, Nicole's limo driver was right. The more he admitted to himself that he loved her, the more he realized that today was not about him. Nicole needed her brother in her life, and he could help her with that.

He turned to Dominic and said, "You go. She needs you. "

Dominic frowned and he looked down at Abby who smiled up at him and nodded. His tone wasn't warm, but for once it wasn't threatening either. "You can ride with us, Stephan. She'll want to see you."

No one moved at first.

Dominic said, "Abby is right. This is about Nicole." When there was still no movement toward the vehicle, Dominic growled, "I get it. Some of this was my fault. I wouldn't have bought your island if I had known how important it was to your family, and I wouldn't have bought your father's company if I had known how good you had all been to Nicole. I really want to hurt you right now, but I won't if my sister loves you. There, can we all get in the limo now?"

For Dominic, that was a downright apology.

A bit tongue in cheek, Stephan answered, "We all make mistakes. I wouldn't have sabotaged your server if I had known that we'd be riding in the same limo one day."

His joke diffused some of the almost visible tension between them.

Jake patted them both on the back, "Right then. Let's go. Everybody in." He herded them into the vehicle and diplomatically sat between them even though they were at least a yard away from each other.

On the drive over, Jake kept looking at the closed window behind the driver. He lowered it and said, "Jeff, right?"

"Yes?"

"You're not Nicole's regular driver, are you?"

"No, I'm covering for my father for the summer."

"You handled that situation back there very well." He handed him his card. "If you want to try your hand at business, give my secretary a call. We've got some entry level positions open."

Jeff laughed and returned the card. "I appreciate the offer, but I'm working on my doctorate in psychology. I wasn't sure what I wanted to do for my internship, but now I'm leaning toward family counseling. It's really much more fascinating than it sounds in books. I thought I'd be bored driving Nicole around, but my dissertation is practically writing itself."

Dominic leaned forward, his voice calm, but laced with deadly intention. "If I see Nicole's name, or any hint of what she shared with you..."

Stephan added his own threat. "You wouldn't have to do anything, Dominic, because he'd already be dead by the time I was done with him."

Abby leaned over and pushed the button for the window to go up and said, "Bye, Jeff. Don't be offended, but I just settled these guys down."

Jeff tossed in a final line just before the window closed. "You might want to consider talking to someone about all this. You could get group rates."

Dominic grumbled, "See, that is the problem with the next generation. Absolutely no respect."

Abby let out a short laugh, then started to really laugh. Jake joined in. Stephan couldn't hold back a smile when even Dominic, a man who had been vying for the world's most miserable billionaire, shook his head in humorous defeat.

"I like him," Abby said, laying a hand on Dominic's thigh.

Dominic rolled his eyes and pulled her closer. "You would."

Nudging an elbow into Dominic side, Abby said, "Come on, group rates? That was hilarious."

Dominic's stern expression melted away when he looked down at Abby's smiling face. "Whose side are you on?"

She leaned over and planted a kiss on his lips. "Yours, Dominic." Then she added, "But that doesn't make it any less funny."

Dominic leaned down and whispered something in her ear and Stephan looked away. Had he lost his chance at that kind of happiness? He wouldn't blame Nicole if she never wanted to see him again, but if she somehow found a way to forgive him, he would make damn sure he was worthy of her this time.

CHAPTER *Twenty-One*

NICOLE ANSWERED THE door of her hotel suite, expecting the room service she'd ordered. Instead, one very chastened billionaire brother filled her doorway.

"Can I come in?" he asked gruffly.

She held the door in her left hand. "I'm not ready to see you yet, Dominic."

He didn't push, and for a man like Dominic that was evidence enough that he was sorry. "I just wanted to make sure you were safe after yesterday."

"What are you afraid I'm going to do?" She blanched at what his expression revealed. "I'm not that upset, Dominic. I'm not going to hurt myself."

His face whitened more and his shoulders rounded. He looked like he hadn't slept in days. He said, "I can't lose you again, Nicole."

182

Nicole moved back so her door opened wider. "Come on in."

They sat on separate couches. Nicole perched nervously on the end of one. Dominic sat with his hands between his knees on another. Nicole asked, "Where did you find Mother?"

He studied her expression and said carefully, "She found me when I took Abby back to the island. She thought I was becoming too much like our father and wanted to save me from myself."

"Where was she all this time?" she asked in a whisper.

"Thomas helped her run to the village where she'd grown up in Italy....then she faked her death, changed her name, and lived on the run until our father died."

"She was that afraid of him?"

"Yes."

"So, it wasn't because she didn't love us?" Nicole bit the inside of her cheek to stop herself from openly crying.

Dominic leaned forward on the couch. "She loved us, Nicole. She still loves us. She genuinely feared for her life—and probably rightfully so. But she wants to see you. She wants to apologize for everything."

Nicole shook her head. "I don't want to see her. Not yet."

Dominic nodded. "I didn't want to either. I didn't think I could forgive her. But she's family, Nicole, and she's the only mother we'll ever have."

Nicole put a shaky hand to her mouth, "I am still so angry with you, Dominic."

He sat back. "I know."

Eyes full of unshed tears, Nicole said, "You were right about Stephan. He didn't love me."

Dominic stood and walked over to join her on the other couch. He touched her arm gently. "No, Nicole. I was wrong about that. He is one incredible pain in my ass -" He stopped abruptly and restarted. "He came to me this morning and told me that he'd used your engagement to keep me distracted while he sabotaged my new server for the Chinese internet."

She sniffed. "See? He used me."

"You're missing the point. He didn't have to tell me. He could have watched me put the server online, and then taken over once China tossed me out. As far as we can tell, no one would have been able to trace it back to him."

"So, why tell you?"

"He did it for you."

Nicole jumped up. "He said that?"

Dominic mouth twisted with distaste. "He did."

"You could have put him in jail."

"That would have been the least of it. He could have lost his company, his reputation, and maybe his life if Abby hadn't intervened." Dominic said, remembering some of his anger.

"He loves me." *He loves me!*

Dominic groaned deep in his chest and said, "Yes."

She announced, "I love him!"

Dominic groaned again. "I know."

She looked around franticly. "I've got to find him."

"He's downstairs in the lobby," Dominic admitted grudgingly.

Nicole's jaw dropped. "You brought him?"

"He came over in the limo with us." Dominic flushed a bit.

Nicole leaned over and hugged Dominic tightly, their first hug in fifteen years. "I can't believe you brought him with you." She leaned back and looked up at her big brother. *You did it for me.* Despite how angry he must have been with Stephan, he had put her needs before his. "You do love me. Who knew you were a big softy under all that roar?"

He smiled down at her, returning her hug so tightly she almost couldn't breathe. "Just don't tell anyone. I'm having a hard enough time commanding respect as it is since I met Abby."

Nicole eased out of the hug and said, "I'm glad you found her."

"I'm a better person when I'm with her."

Nicole nodded. "I feel that way when I'm with Stephan and his family. I feel like nothing can touch me. I'm free to be the person I was meant to be."

Dominic took her hand, "I was wrong to come between you and the Andrades. I was scared."

Nicole blinked quickly with shock. "Scared? You?"

Dominic met her eyes, not proud of what he had done, but not hiding from it either. His tone was somewhat detached, but she saw now that distancing himself from the pain was how he'd survived. "I had meant to come back for you as soon as I thought I was strong enough to defend you against our father. One year became three, then four. You refused to have any contact with me. I kept thinking that everything would change after I found Mom. When news came that she was dead, I went crazy. I was angry with our father, angry with our dead mother, angry with you for seeming to accept it all. Then you found the Andrades and moved on like they were your new family. But you already had a family. You had me. I knew when I bought their company that it would drive a wedge between you and them. I knew it and I convinced myself it was for the best."

185

Nicole squeezed her brother's hand. "You and I have some serious separation-anxiety issues." Dominic opened his mouth to say something but Nicole spoke over him. "It's ok, Dominic. Now is what matters." A thought came to her and she added, "But please don't assign any body guards to me now that we're talking again. You're a little over the top with that."

"I protect what is mine."

"You're my brother, Dominic. Nothing will ever change that, but I also love the Andrades. You'll have to respect that. And I won't go back to being sheltered from the world. If you want to be part of my life, you're going to have to trust that I can take care of myself."

"I will. I do." He blushed and conceded the truth. "I'll try."

Speaking of Andrades, Nicole asked, "Now where did you say Stephan was?"

And without waiting for Dominic's answer, Nicole bolted out the door and into the elevator.

STEPHAN STOPPED, MID-PACE when he saw Nicole step out of the elevator. He held his breath and waited. Was this the end or the beginning?

She crossed the foyer to him. Dammit, he should have met her halfway, but her expression was difficult to read and he couldn't unfreeze his feet. She stopped a foot in front of him and said, "You lied to me."

He swallowed hard. "Yes."

"And you used me."

There was no reason to lie anymore. "Yes."

"And you really sabotaged Dominic's server?"

He simply nodded. Waiting.

186

"So why aren't you out celebrating your victory? Why did you confess?"

She knew. She knew why he'd done it. He cleared his throat. "Because I love you."

She leaned in, cupping her ear, with a mischievous sparkle in her gorgeous gray eyes. "I'm sorry. What was that? I didn't hear you."

He pulled her to him, linking his hands behind her back, thankful for the millionth time that she'd given up her heavy pants suits for thin sundresses. "You heard me."

Not ready yet to let him off the hook, she shook her head with mock sadness, "Well, if you can't even say it in public, how am I going to believe you?"

Stephan stepped back and up onto the coffee table in the foyer. "Excuse me everyone," His voice carried the authority to turn all the heads in the area. He pointed down at Nicole. "I love this woman. If she is willing to marry me, we are going to fill a huge house with tons of kids, and I am going to spend the rest of my life proving to her that she was right to forgive me."

Nicole blushed the most beautiful shade of pink and said, "Everyone is looking, Stephan."

He reached down and dragged her up onto the table with him. "Well, then this is the perfect time for me to ask you." He got down on one knee. "Will you marry me?"

She looked down at her left hand which no longer wore his ring. "How do I know this is real? How do I know this isn't just one more game?"

He reached into his coat pocket and pulled out a small ring, less than a carat, in an antique setting. "This was my grandmother's ring. My mother wore it when she was engaged to my father and hopefully, one day, our daughter will wear it. I'm done playing games. Marry me, Nicole, and let me prove that to you."

She only made him suffer for the longest moment of his life before saying, "Yes. Yes, I will marry you." She offered him her hand and he slid the ring on her finger.

They lost themselves in a kiss while the crowd cheered.

Eventually, coming back to earth, Stephan stepped down from the table with a huge smile. He held up a hand to help Nicole step down.

Abby said, "It looks like they made up, Dominic."

Dominic growled, "I can see that."

Jake said, "You're going to have to forgive him."

Dominic made a threatening sound deep in his throat.

Stephan joined them. No matter what had come before today, this was Nicole's brother. Stephan held out his hand to Dominic. "I'm sorry, Dominic. I was wrong, and I let what I thought I knew about you guide me to some reprehensible behavior. I hope we can work this out."

When Dominic didn't move, Abby jabbed him with her elbow. He looked down at her and said, "How am I ever going to scare anyone if you keep doing that?"

Abby smiled up at him.

Stephan laughed. "I don't think it will be a problem."

Dominic's expression remained serious. "If you're good to my sister, you will never have anything to fear from me."

Jake piped in, "See, Dom, that's the kind of comment that makes people wonder what you're capable of. Couldn't you just shake his hand and accept his apology?"

Dominic did shake Stephan's hand and the two of them reached an unspoken understanding in that moment.

For Nicole.

LATER THAT DAY, Nicole stepped out of her shoes as she entered their penthouse. Stephan closed the door behind him and swept her up into his arms. She wrapped her arms around his neck and couldn't stop smiling.

He nuzzled her cheek and said, "We're finally alone and we've resolved all of our issues. Do you know what this means?"

His kisses tickled her neck. She knew exactly what it meant, but she decided to have a little fun. "You want me to cook again?"

He tossed her down on the couch and shed his jacket. He shook his head, a predatory smile spreading across his face.

"You've recorded a program that you'd like to watch together?" she asked impishly.

He loosened his tie and threw it on the floor behind him. Without taking his eyes off her, he slowly, deliberately began to unbutton his shirt. Nicole's mouth dried and her stomach quivered. He dropped his shirt behind him, standing tall and proud, fully aware of the effect his muscled torso was having on her blood pressure.

Nicole gripped the cushion beneath her. *God, he was beautiful.*

Slowly, so slowly that she wanted to jump up and do it for him, Stephan undid his leather belt and unbuttoned the top of his trousers. With a flick of the zipper, he slid his pants down and stepped out of them. His dark blue boxers did little to conceal his excitement.

Nicole's body clenched and shivered in response to every move Stephan made. He walked toward where she sat and leaned in, kneeling beside her on the couch, his warm breath hot against her ear. She shivered again, but didn't move. Ever so softly, he purred, "Step One: The Shake Up. Would you say that I have your full attention now?"

Nicole pulled back with a surprised laugh. "You know about that, too?"

"Don't tell the women, but the men have always known." He looped a finger beneath the strap of her dress and moved it aside, exposing a bare shoulder to his eager lips. "My father warned me about the notorious bikini scenario, but I never thought I'd actually experience it."

He tasted her collar-bone, making it difficult for Nicole to focus on what he was saying, but as the image of that day replayed in her head, she swatted him playfully. "You could have said something."

"And miss the fun? How would I know what to warn our sons about?" He slid her other strap down and gave that shoulder equal attention.

Nicole closed her eyes and threw her head back in pleasure. One strong, confident hand lifted her, while the other expertly slipped beneath her dress and removed her panties. Her eyes flew open and met his.

God, he was hot.

He pulled the dress up and over her head in a single move and laid her down on the couch naked and exposed. He ran one light finger across her lips, down her neck, through the valley between her small breasts, down her stomach. He whispered, "Tell me what you like."

Barely able to breath, Nicole admitted, "I don't really know."

He stopped and she feared she'd ruined the moment. Self-recriminations were just finding their voice, when he said, "Then that's where we'll start."

190

He rolled onto the couch with her so they lay face to face. He laid one hand on her hip and said, "Kiss me."

Nicole closed the short distance between their mouths and quickly forgot why she'd been embarrassed. His lips caressed and worshipped. His tongue teased and suggested. She met his moves with her own and together they explored the passion that they'd both tried so long to deny.

His mouth moved down her neck and Nicole's body sprung to life wherever he kissed. His hands were firm, but gentle. Just when she thought she couldn't take anymore, he would pause and wait, giving her time to counter with her own explorations.

She removed his boxers impatiently and reveled in the hard excitement that pulsed in her hand. She encircled and stroked, awed at how his body jerked with pleasure at her touch. His uninhibited desire for her gave her the confidence to let herself go and enjoy. Simply enjoy.

His hand found her wet center. His thumb settled on her clitoris and rubbed a rhythm she felt clear down to her toes. One magical finger slid inside of her, working in union with his other finger to drive all coherent thought out of her mind. When she was writhing beneath him, jutting against his hand, begging him not to stop, he replaced his hand with his mouth. The heat of climax spread through her, leaving her a shuddering mass at his mercy.

His smile promised that instead of being the end, this was merely the beginning.

Gently, he rolled her onto her stomach and pushed her hair aside, drawing a path with one hand, and following that path with his lips. He caressed each inch of her, lovingly, passionately, until the last thing she wanted was to be facing away from him. And still, his hands stroked her. Bringing every corner of her alive for him.

When she could take no more, she rolled over, sending both of them onto the floor. He broke her fall easily. His strong arms raised her above his excitement, holding her poised and ready as his tip jerked beneath her, waiting to be taken within her. "Show me what you like, Nicole."

Nicole lowered herself on him, savoring how he filled her. She moved tentatively at first like a dancer who had never taken the lead. Testing. Clenching when she discovered the secret to her own pleasure and loving how he met her move for move.

With Stephan she was free – even here. Free to be who she'd always wanted to be. And she let herself go to fully enjoy the rhythm they found together. Their shared orgasm left them spent and still connected, hugging each other while their breathing slowly returned to normal.

Nicole raised her head slightly and kissed Stephan softly on the mouth. She said, "You can put all of that on the list of what I like."

He smiled against her lips and said, "I'm going to enjoy adding to that list."

Nicole flexed her inner muscles around him and felt him harden within her. "Me, too." She said, "Me, too."

He cupped her bare ass with his hands and began to move her hips in a circular motion, taking them both to a place where communication did not require any words.

THE NEXT DAY, Nicole and Stephan returned to their morning ritual of having breakfast together. The beauty of it brought a shine of emotion to Nicole's eyes. Beyond their passion, beyond the depth of their love for each other, they were also friends, and that was what gave Nicole the strength to believe that they could make it.

Stephan took a bite of his toast and asked as casually as if he were inquiring about the weather, "What do you think about buying a house in California and living there part of the year?"

"I would love that," Nicole gushed. "Are you considering making documentaries again?"

Stephan nodded. "Mark gave me the hard sell while I was there and he made some good points. I could also take it a step further than making movies, and challenge a few of my competitors to go *green*. I hate to say that your brother has set another example for me, but his substantial investment in scholarship funds, both here and in China, set the stage for large companies to follow suit. There are countless major corporations out there now looking for high profile causes. I could spotlight those causes for them."

"Speaking of my brother..." Nicole wasn't quite sure how Stephan would respond to her idea, but it was something she desperately wanted to make happen. "I'd like to invite Dominic and Abby to dinner this Sunday with your family."

Stephan squeezed her hand gently, "Your brother might not love my family as much as you do."

"He will," Nicole said simply.

"When did you become so optimistic?" Stephan asked with a pleased smile.

"Since I started believing in happy endings."

Stephan cocked one eyebrow at her, not yet understanding what she was talking about.

"All the major holidays will be here before we know it. I never really celebrated them before and this year I want everyone to be together. That's only going to happen if they get to know each other. If you called Dominic and invited him, he would come." He still looked doubtful, so she added a heartfelt "Pleeeeease."

Stephan scratched his chin in serious consideration, then said, "Maybe you should ask me again while wearing that little red bikini."

Nicole laughed and threw a napkin at him. "You're an ass."

He grinned and said, "Yes, but I'm an ass who is going to call your brother because I love you."

Nicole walked around the small table, sat in Stephan's lap and gave him the kind of kiss that makes a man late for work.

A FEW HOURS later, Stephan left, and Nicole made some phone calls before texting Jeff to pick her up for the drive to her father's house.

She flew past Jeff in a rush and slid into the limo. She was late and she was never late. It was impossible not to blush every few minutes when she thought about why.

Bubbling over with happiness, Nicole spontaneously pressed the button to lower the partition between the front and back seat and said, "Jeff, you were so right about everything! I'm glad I waited to have sex with Stephan. Last night was everything I've always dreamt of, and I have to thank you for that."

Not sure exactly what response she expected, Nicole went from pink to bright red when Jeff's father, Arnold, peered back at her from the driver's seat. "I got home last night, Miss Corisi," he said in his most professional tone.

Nicole scrambled to organize her thoughts and spoke before she had completed the process. "Oh. Well, tell Jeff I said thank you."

Arnold stared back at her in the rearview mirror and said nothing.

"Or not." Nicole buried her face in one hand and fought back a smile. Poor Arnold. "This is the kind of moment we can probably pretend didn't happen, right?"

Arnold started the engine. "Yes, Miss Corisi," he said, sounding a bit relieved. "Do you want to go directly to the house?"

"No, I promised Maddy and Abby that I would pick them up on the way. They are going to help me sort my father's belongings." She gave him their addresses.

"That's nice that you don't have to do it alone," Arnold said, breaking his near twenty-year rule of keeping their exchanges completely impersonal.

Reflecting on his comment, Nicole's smile spread from ear to ear. Even if it made him uncomfortable, she had to tell him how much better her life had gotten while he'd been gone. Her voice was thick with gratitude. "I'm not alone anymore, Arnold. I have a family now."

Arnold looked away, but she saw in the mirror that his eyes were misty. "That's good, Nicole."

A flash of inspiration hit Nicole. "You know what else is good?"

He looked back at her before pulling into traffic.

"A raise. A big, fat raise that will let you take your wife on a trip every year."

He said, "You don't have to do that, Nicole."

No, I don't have to, but I want to. She teased, "Oh, you'll earn it, Arnold. Wait till you meet Stephan's nephews."

"Hellions?" he asked with a pleased smile.

"And fast."

Arnold surprised her more by saying, "You deserve to be happy, Nicole."

Nicole put her hand through the opening that separated them and gave his shoulder an affectionate squeeze. "I don't know if I deserve to be, but I am, Arnold. I finally am."

Nicole could have sworn he flushed a little. She sat back in her seat with a happy, albeit tearful grin. "I'm going to put up the divider now, Arnold, so you can have some peace."

"Thank you, Miss Corisi," he said, returning to formality.

Before cutting off their brief connection, Nicole added something that needed to be voiced, "Thank you for not leaving me, Arnold."

He didn't say anything, but Nicole caught a glimpse of his smile just before the window blocked him from view.

I always felt so alone, but I guess I never really was.

Arnold was about to become the best paid limo driver in New York City.

CHAPTER *Twenty-Two*

MADDY'S HUSBAND, RICHARD, was full-on creating his Sunday feast for the Andrade clan, threatening anyone who so much as dared to lift a cover to one of the many pots.

Abby sipped the coffee she'd gladly accepted a few moments ago from Katrine. "When you invited me over early to cook I imagined…well, cooking."

Elise waved a hand at the man in the background who was cursing his creations in French and said, "Today is Richard's day to cook. We just come in here to get away from the men so we can really talk."

Nicole shared a knowing look with Abby. "I know. I thought the same thing when they invited me. Seemed a little sexist to have all the women in the kitchen while the men stayed out in the living room, but this is where all the good stuff happens."

Maddy laid Joseph back in his rolling bassinet. "I grew up like this, but I confess that in my teens I thought I was missing something by not being out there. Remember that year, Mom?"

Elise smiled and said, "Oh, yes. I remember. It didn't take you long to realize that all the important decisions are made in here."

Nicole asked with laughter in her voice, "Do the men know that?"

Abby had a more serious question. "It's your choice to be in here, though, isn't it? I mean if you wanted to sit out there and talk they would let you, right?"

Elise nodded reassuringly. "Oh, don't worry. You're welcome to go out there and soak in as much microchip design and marketing platform talk as you can stomach. Just leave me in here."

The look of surprise on Abby's face made the older woman smile. "Abby, the women's rights movement was about equality so we could choose who we want to be, not so we could all become men or software designers. I don't bring in an income anymore, but I am on several charities and I consider my family a full-time job. Alessandro would support me if I wanted to run part of the company, but I'm not interested. The great part about getting older is you realize that you don't have to impress anyone else. I'm happy with things just the way they are."

Katrine added, "I have to agree. Victor and I worked hard for many years to make Andrade Solutions successful. He used to say I could negotiate the wings off a fly if I had to, and sometimes finding new vendors was that difficult. Not all the years were profitable ones. We worked because we had to, but you ladies are lucky enough to be able to follow your passions."

Abby squared her shoulders and said, "I have to admit, I'm not totally sure what to do with myself now. I always worked a day job. Sometimes two. I can't really go back to teaching in the inner city schools. Dominic would have a swat team following me at all times. How do you not lose yourself around men who cast such a large shadow?"

Elise leaned over and laid a supportive hand on Abby's. "You stand beside them and make your own path. There is a price to wealth, but there is also a freedom that comes with it. As a teacher, you touched the lives of a few hundred. Now, you could touch the lives of millions if you wanted to. The wonderful thing about our men is if you want it, they will help you make it happen. Dominic seems like he's that same kind of good man."

Safe within a group of women who genuinely cared about her, Nicole shared, "Until I met Stephan, I didn't see any good in having money. I resented the importance people placed on things and appearances. I don't know that I ever spent a moment being grateful for what I had. In Stephan's eyes, everyone is connected whether it is through our environment or our finances, and the more you have, the more responsible you should be. When you look at the world like that, it's hard not to want to get involved in every cause. I'm going to focus on helping abused women put their lives back together. From what you've shared with me, Abby, you might want to focus on education and reform. There must have been policies you dealt with as a teacher that you felt powerless to change. Now you have a voice."

Maddy sighed. "I love happy endings."

Nicole said, "As a wise limo driver once told me, the story doesn't end when the book does. This is just the beginning for us. For all of us."

Abby looked at the door and said, "Speaking of all of us, how do you think the men are getting along?"

Katrine wasn't concerned. "The boys will play nice. Alessandro and Victor are in there. "

Nicole laughed. "Babysitting two of the biggest egos on the planet."

Smiling, Katrine said, "Where do you think Stephan got his ego? Victor was quite a stinker when I first met him, but our forty-plus years of marriage have domesticated him."

Her words seemed to touch a cord in Abby. She asked, "Do you have any advice on how to make it last?"

Katrine said, "Honesty. Respect. Forgiveness."

Elise joked, "And a little red bikini."

Nicole sat up straight, remembering something. "Oh," she said loudly, then lowered her voice. "*they* know about the red bikini. The Steps are no longer a secret."

Elise and Katrine spun in union to look accusingly at Richard, but he didn't look up from stirring his sauce. Just as quickly, they turned back and said, "Maddy!"

A sheepish smile spread across the younger woman's face. She shrugged.

Laughing, Nicole shook her head. "You are so bad."

Maddy wiggled her eyebrows at Nicole. "Difficult to stay mad, though, isn't it, when my meddling brought you and Stephan back together?"

Abby sat back in her chair with a huge smile on her face. "Nicole, I totally understand why you love this family." She turned to Elise and asked, "Would you mind if I brought my sister, Lil, to dinner sometime? She needs this."

Nicole had gotten to know Abby pretty well over the last few days and she knew how much she loved and worried about her sister. Nicole asked, "How is she? Has she spoken to Jake since that day on the island? Didn't you say you thought there was a connection there? Maybe you could invite them both. Would that be ok?" Nicole looked at the two older women at the table.

Katrine said, "Abby, your family is our family. Invite them."

Elise said, "Jake. Jake." She repeated his name as if trying to conjure up his image in her mind. "Isn't he Dominic's partner?" Nicole and Abby nodded. Elise clapped her hands together once. "He's beautiful and outrageously wealthy. How wonderful would that be if he and your sister got married?"

Abby's eyes rounded, realizing that she just might have started something she wasn't sure she could contain. "Thank you for saying that, Katrine. I will bring Lil. Now, Jake, I don't know about. He and Lil haven't stayed in touch as far as I know. Maybe we should just let them figure it out."

Maddy waved two excited hands in the air. "I have the *perfect* idea on how to get them together."

"No!" everyone said in chorus.

Putting one indignant hand on a hip, Maddy said, "*When* will you appreciate my genius?"

Nicole nodded grudgingly. "I have to admit, I'm happy with your results."

"See," Maddy stressed, pointing to her recent success case. "Sometimes love just happens, but other times it needs a little push."

Elise leaned toward her daughter, "What are you hatching up in that little head of yours this time?"

Maddy turned to Abby, "Do you think Dominic can be trusted?"

A wicked smile lit Abby's normally sweet face. "If it means feeding Jake a little humble pie, I'd say absolutely."

Maddy said, "This is going to be awesome."

"Maddy," Katrine started in a firm, warning-laced tone that took a little of the wind out of her niece's sails. Maddy's arms dropped to her sides and she turned to her aunt, accepting the anticipated admonishment. After a pause, Katrine changed her mind. She leaned over and hugged her niece and said, "Don't ever change."

Hesitating only for a moment to reflect on Katrine's words, Maddy quickly regained her enthusiasm. "Ok, this is what I think we should do…"

TO STEPHAN'S SURPRISE, Dominic had driven himself to the house. No wingman. No security. Just Abby.

Another man would have been nervous about being so clearly outnumbered, but Dominic entered the Andrade household with his head held high. He shook Victor and Alessandro's hands without hesitation. He paused, but did not refuse to shake Stephan's.

Alessandro led them through the house and asked his staff to bring them coffee outside. Three Andrade men and one Corisi sat on the large patio that overlooked acres of freshly cut lawn.

Once the men were seated, Victor said, "Your sister is already like a daughter to me. I was pleased that you accepted our invitation."

Dominic nodded in acknowledgement of the statement, then looked over at Stephan. "Abby explained to me that you thought I had swindled your father out of his company and Isola Santos."

Stephan looked at his future brother-in-law right in the eye and said, "That's true."

Dominic added, "But now you know the truth."

Stephan acknowledged he did with a slight incline of his head.

Neither man blinked.

Dominic said, "Had the situation been reversed, I would have done exactly what you did. And you almost beat me. Not many people can say that."

The air stilled. Stephan said, "I'm not proud of what I did."

"That could be the title of my own memoir," Dominic said ruefully. Then a bit more seriously, he said, "Abby is right. We can't change the past, but we don't have to repeat it either. Be good to my sister, Stephan."

"I will be," Stephan said, seeing clearly for the first time the love Dominic had for Nicole.

Dominic reached into his pocket and pulled out an envelope. He handed it to Victor. "This is the deed to Isola Santos. I want you to have it."

Victor looked at the two proud men before him and said, "Why don't you make it a wedding present for Stephan and Nicole so that our legacy is a blending of our families?"

Dominic re-pocketed the deed and cleared his throat. "I'd like that."

Alessandro leaned forward in his seat and asked, "So, have you made any progress debugging your server?"

Victor shook his head at his brother in disapproval.

Alessandro countered, "We're family now, no? How are we going to help him if we don't discuss it?"

Family. At the end of the day, that's what Dominic was now. Stephan said, "Dominic, you're welcome to use the software design I was going to offer China."

Dominic shook his head. "Not an option. It's different enough that they would know. And, unfortunately, your hacker knew what he was doing, Stephan. No one I've paid an obscene amount of hush money to has been able to fix it. It's as if the virus attached to every line of code."

Victor looked at his son and said, "Stephan, with all of your connections, you don't know anyone who could help?"

With a one-shoulder shrug, Stephan said, "The only man I knew who was that good was the man who created the virus, and he's not budging."

Dominic said, "I know of some people who could defrag God if they wanted, but I'm not sure they would help us."

Stephan stood. "Whatever you need, Dominic. If it's money…"

"No, they don't care about money."

Stephan said, "Everyone has their price. What do they care about?"

"Jake," Dominic answered.

Victor stood up. "No, Jake isn't one of *those* Waltons, is he?"

Stephan asked, "What are you talking about, Dad?"

"In the late 1980's, two highly-respected computer designers made the news for claiming their software was being stolen by the US government for military purposes. It was a huge scandal that ended so abruptly that people were taking bets on whether they'd been bought out or brutally silenced. Either way, it was a loss. The quantum encryption software they were working on back then was so far

204

advanced that we still use their notes as a guide today. If they are alive and still working on software design, I want to meet them. You think Jake is their son?"

Dominic shifted in his chair like he'd been caught saying much more than he'd meant to. "He's never admitted to it, but I believe he is."

Victor stood and joined Stephan by the stone railing. "Looks like we're going to have to find out. Dominic, how much time do you have left before your server goes online?"

"About a month," Dominic said.

Stephan said, "That's not much time."

Alessandro patted his nephew's shoulder in support and said, "I know some people who might be able to help us track them down. If they are alive, I'll have their location within a week."

Sweaty and still in his kitchen apron, Richard opened the door to the patio with a huge smile and said, "Dominic, your presence is being requested in the kitchen."

Dominic looked around at the other men who were also suspiciously smiling. Alessandro walked over and gave Dominic a sympathetic pat on the back. "It's never a good sign."

Victor joked, "Maybe they have an extra apron."

Dominic wordlessly appealed to Stephan for help. Stephan gave him no sympathy, just a wicked smile. "The mighty Dominic Corisi cowers before a kitchen of women?"

Not denying the accusation, Dominic growled, "If you think it's so funny, you go see what they want."

Stephan hopped up onto the wide stone railing and didn't attempt to hide his amusement. "They asked for *you*."

Dominic headed into the house, tossing a threat over his shoulder. "I'll remember this, Stephan."

Turning back to his father and uncle, Stephan said, "What do you think they want to see him for?"

Alessandro shrugged. "I'll ask Maddy later."

Stephan shook his head with humor, then a thought came to him. "Dad, I have one more confession." Both older men went absolutely still and Stephan wished he had chosen his words more carefully. He hoped he never had another of *those* confessions. This one was much easier to share. "I told Nicole that we know about the red bikini scam."

Victor said sadly, "Now your mother won't wear hers anymore."

"Dad!" Stephan jumped off the railing and tried to block out the mental image his father had just scarred him with.

Ever optimistic, Alessandro said, "Maybe they'll come up with something even better. Although, I will miss Elise meeting me at the door in hers."

Time to go. "I'm going to see if Dominic needs me."

Stephan stopped at the door of the kitchen and took in the scene before him. Richard had returned to his post at the stove. Maddy was enthusiastically laying out some wild scheme to Dominic whose entire demeanor was softer here with the women. Dominic looked across at Abby, shared a laugh with her and nodded in agreement with something Elise said.

One month. They had one month to fix Dominic's server.

We can do it. He thought. *We have to.*

Nicole caught a glimpse of him and headed over to his side. She hugged him, and the weight of the world slid off his shoulders. She said, "The rest of the family will be here soon. How did it go out there? You're both still alive and smiling, so I'm guessing it went ok."

"My father liked him, I could tell. And Uncle Alessandro is going to locate someone who could help him remove the virus."

Nicole turned her face into Stephan's shirt and he felt her shudder against him. He eased her back a little so he could see her expression. "What is it, Nicole? I'd thought you'd be happy."

Fighting back tears, she said huskily, "I *am* happy. I'm so happy that I'm afraid. Can this really be my life? What if I wake up and none of this happened?"

He tucked a stray lock behind her ear and said, "If you do, come to my office in Manhattan. I'm sitting there with your photo in my desk, waiting for you."

Then he kissed her, the kind of kiss that makes an overprotective brother growl something from across the room, and a crazy aunt give a standing ovation.

THE *End*

If you enjoyed Nicole and Stephan, please look for:

Maid for the Billionaire (Book One) – Abby and Dominic

Bedding the Billionaire (Summer, 2012) - Lil and Jake

Saving the Sheik (Summer, 2013) - Zhang and a sheik (Because imagining a sheik kidnapping a woman like Zhang is just too much fun not to write about!)

If you'd like to contact the author, you can find Ruth Cardello on Facebook at Author Ruth Cardello or you can email her via her website at www.ruthiecardello.com.

EXTRA SCENE

The following scene was contributed by a reader in Ohio, Karen Lawson. She is a retired school teacher, a wife, a mother and a grandmother. Karen originally met me through my author Facebook page, but has become a friend along the way.

I held a contest in September of 2011. Readers were encouraged to write scenes loosely related to either Maid for the Billioniare or For Love or Legacy. Although her writing will not be incorporated into the actual storyline, it is well written and entertaining to read.

So, please take a few moments to enjoy my characters through the eyes of one of their fans:

Jeff's doctoral dissertation won him much acclaim. He received his Ph.D. in psychology the spring after his adventure with Nicole. When Dr. Jeff started his counseling practice an invitation was sent to the Corisi/Andrade/Dartley family for a complementary group session. They were - of course - the reason his dissertation had been such a triumph.

After many scheduling conflicts and days of phone tag, the day finally arrived. Arnold graciously chauffeured the group of fifteen to his son's new spacious office complex.

The large facility had been recently remodeled with Arnold's help thanks to the huge bonus Nicole had given him. Because Nicole wasn't using Arnold during the day, he had had time to help Jeff design a state of the art facility that catered to family groups. The innovative center housed a fully-staffed childcare station and three enormous group rooms.

As the group entered the building, the small children - Colby clutching Joey's hand - headed straight for the childcare room. Lil and Maddy followed closely behind to make sure their sons were checked in with the staff. Victor and Katrine accompanied Rosella to the first group room. Elise and Alessandro walked behind them with Richard closely trailing. Dominic, hand in hand with Abby, entered with Jake to bring up the rear. Several minutes later Nicole and Stephan rushed in looking a bit frazzled, but smiling. Arnold was behind them letting his son know that he tried to hurry them out of the limo, but as they were the last to leave, it took them a bit longer to exit. Victor and Katrine shared a knowing glance, remembering young love. Finally Lil and Maddy entered from the side door closest to the daycare station.

Nicole was still having problems warming up to her mother; one of the reasons Dr. Jeff had requested this session. In fact, there were so many issues with all these people that Jeff had everyone sit in a circle and proceeded to ask each one to communicate any problems they felt they had.

"Well," said Nicole, "I'll start. I know you think my mother is my real issue. You are probably right, but there are some other things that I need to talk about. Ever since I made millions selling Dad's estate, Abby and I can't decide how to decorate the Abuse Center."

"That's right," answered Abby. "I'm not sure I even want to continue with the Abuse Center. I'm trying to find a charity that will meet my needs too. How about Inner School Reading Programs?"

210

Lil chimed in. "I'm so tired of hearing all about my soon-to-be-rich sister! I am a single parent still supporting Colby in our small house, while she is living in the lap of luxury. How come I can't have a great story too?"

"Oh don't worry about that Lil," said Jake. "There are many things you have yet to learn about me. When we have our time, you will be well taken care of, just wait! I just want to get to the rest of this saga!"

"How about our whole problem in China?" whined Dominic. "We only have a limited amount of time before the servers start. If it wasn't for Stephan, this wouldn't be a problem!"

"Are you kidding? I am trying to help, but you have threatened me so much with your sister that I have to keep her happy," retorted Stephan. "All she wants to talk about is wedding plans."

"I can understand that," replied Dominic. "Maybe we should all elope and just get these weddings over with. I think there is a possibility that Abby could be pregnant."

"Pregnant?" exclaimed Rosella. "Can I finally be a grandmother?"

"You can't even be a mother!" whispered Nicole.

"Dominic, that is not your story to tell now! Besides, we still need to figure out how we can split Isola Santos with Nicole and Stephan. I think they should take down the garish steel and glass monstrosity and we should remodel the 18th century castle," hinted Abby.

Victor piped in, "If Stephan and Nicole will be moving to the island, Katrine and I won't have to move back here to see our future grandchildren."

"That would be great," contended Alessandro. "Our house has become party central with all of you. Elise and I would like some alone time. Ever since Maddy blabbed about the Step Solution, I haven't seen my wife in a bikini. Then again, with Richard cooking all the time, she doesn't look that great in one anymore."

"See if I will make dinner for you anymore!" exclaimed Richard. "You can have your Italian cooking. Joey and Maddy and I will eat fine French cuisine without you! Now that I think about it, his name is back to Laurent."

"Stop!" screamed Abby. "We all sound like a bunch of children. We love each other. Katrine once said that 'love is a decision to care about someone even when you want to strangle them and forgive them for not being perfect.' I think we can all say that no one here is perfect. And I for one would like to strangle a few of you right now."

Dr. Jeff finally spoke. "Let's get back on track. Rosella, how do you feel about how you treated your children?"

"I love my children, and I can see that I did the wrong thing. However, Thomas and I have recently started seeing each other and I think I am madly in love with him. We want to run away and live in Italy. The children can come visit us whenever."

"I think you all need another session with me. It is true that 'life doesn't stop when the book ends.' We may need a whole new novel for all of you!" said Dr. Jeff.

Extra scene © Katherine Lawson, 2011
reprinted with permission

Made in the USA
Middletown, DE
29 September 2015